SAME T

"Jesus, that was *incredible*, wasn't it? Really *incredible*."

"It was . . . nice." Doris smiled.

George cocked his head.

"Especially the last time," she added quickly.

He winced. "I know—I'm an animal! Jesus!" George threw his second shoe at the wall and paced, berating himself, to the window. Christ, if Kinsey had interviewed *him*—"I don't know—I don't know what got *into* me," he said. "I just—" He frowned, and suddenly turned. "What was the matter with the first two times?"

"Hmmm?" She was busy gathering clothes. She gave his questions serious thought. "Well. The first time was kind of fast, and the second—" She stopped. "You really want to hear this? I mean, I feel funny talking about it."

"It was very, very beautiful, Doris. There was nothing dirty or disgusting in what we did."

She nodded slowly, watching his face. "Then how come you look so down in the dumps?"

He nodded slowly. "Because my wife's gonna *kill* me, Doris."

LINDA STEWART

Same Time, Next Year

A novel based on
the stageplay and screenplay
by
Bernard Slade

FONTANA/Collins

First published in the United States by Dell Publishing Co. Inc. 1978
First published in Great Britain by Fontana Books 1979

This novelization by Linda Stewart is based on the play, copyright © 1975 by Bernard Slade, and the screenplay.
Novelization copyright © 1978 by Bernard Slade

Made and printed in Great Britain by
William Collins Sons & Co Ltd, Glasgow

All rights reserved. No part of this book may be reproduced or transmitted in any form or by any means, electronic or mechanical, including photocopying, recording, or by any information storage and retrieval system, without the written permission of the Publisher, except where permitted by law.

CONDITIONS OF SALE
This book is sold subject to the condition that it shall not, by way of trade or otherwise, be lent, re-sold, hired out or otherwise circulated without the publisher's prior consent in any form of binding or cover other than that in which it is published and without a similar condition including this condition being imposed on the subsequent purchaser

APPOINTMENTS

Friday, Feb. 23, 1951

9AM - Flight 121
Idlewild

Sea Shadows Inn

G. Peters

GEORGE

ONE

It was snowing softly in Clifton, New Jersey, but George was resting on tropic sand. The air around him was warm and clear, deeply scented with red hibiscus, faintly humming with harmless bees.

George awakened, slightly dazed. He opened his eyes, but lay without moving for several seconds, staring blankly through tousled hair, letting the clock continue to buzz—an electric saw, amputating the tail of his dream.

What was the dream . . .? He couldn't recall. In the predawn purple-dark of the room he tried to pursue it. Lost. Gone. Sighing softly, George shook his head and fumbled around for his first cigarette.

Helen slept.

"Hey?" he whispered.

Helen slept.

George sighed.

The alarm continued to cut through the air.

George turned it off and the radio on. It blatted loudly of Rinso White. George got up. Helen slept. Helen, he reflected, was the kind of woman who could sleep through anything, except for the faint cough of a child as heard through a thirty-foot granite wall. George, who completely adored his children, wished, at times, they would just disappear, and leave him, at times, with a girl named Helen, a gorgeous sophomore at NYU who'd said to an unremarkable soldier on a 48-hour pass in New York, "I think I've waited all my life for you, George." She'd said it in the lobby of the Paramount Theatre, a quarter way into their first blind date. Exactly a week after that, they were married. Exactly a month after that, she was pregnant, and several days after that, he was gone—shipped to England to meet with his war. By the time he came home, Helen was gone, replaced by a Wonderful Wife And Mother. A *wonderful* wife; a *wonderful* mother; everything a fortunate fellow could want—unless he just wanted a girl named Helen.

Rubbing his eyes, George moved away, crossing the bedroom to look at the snow, and promptly tripped on the packed suitcase that sat in the middle of the carpeted floor. "GOD*DAMMIT*!" he managed to yell as his toes recorded the Terrible Pain.

He looked at Helen.

Helen slept.

At the bathroom sink he splashed at his face and shoveled Ipana into his mouth. Through the open doorway, the radio jeered:

Another terrible Friday morning at the terrible hour of 5 A.M. and driving conditions are TERRIBLE, folks.

George reached out for the Listerine.

In Korea the country remains at war, and defense-mobilizer Charles E. Wilson stated, "What's good for General Motors is good for the country."

George thought it over, gargled, and spat.

An atomic shelter, the first in the nation, was early yesterday evening installed in the yard of a Mr. and Mrs. Fish of Bayswell, Florida. Said Mrs. Fish:

"It was only two thousand dollars, you know? So Herm's gonna buy me another mink coat, so I said to him Herm will you LISten to me Herm, what good, God forbid, would the FIRST mink be if I'm dead of radiation, you know what I mean?"

George started shaving.

"Daddy?" Michael stood on the sill, unhooking the door of his Dr. Dentons. "What's radiation?" Michael yawned.

"Disease. You catch it from kissing radios."

"Kissing *radios*?" Michael giggled.

"*Strange* radios," George explained.

Michael seemed to be giving it thought. Michael was seven and looked like George, except he was pale, blond, and myopic. Also, he was terribly short for his age. George loved him in a way that was painful.

Michael was hooking his Dr. Dentons again. "Who'd kiss a *radio*?" Michael protested.

"Someone who's very, very horny and please don't ask me what horny is."

Another movie opens tonight—Bedtime For Bonzo, *with Ronald Reagan.*

"Oh, I bet it's like s-e-x." Michael had closed the lid of the john and stood on it, watching George as he shaved. "Can I be horny when I grow up?"

"Probably." George studied his son. "If you're good," he added, and suddenly laughed.

Michael frowned, and stepped from the lid to the top of the tank. "If it sticks, will you take me sledding tomorrow?"

"You know I'll be in California tomorrow. . . . You want a ride to the kitchen?"

"Yeah. I guess." Michael climbed onto George's back. George felt the weight. "Are you getting older," he said, "or am I?"

"I hate that," Michael said in the hall, "when you give me those answers I don't understand. About s-e-x."

"S-e-x," George repeated, "is something *no*body understands."

"Why are you going to California?"

George set his son on the kitchen counter, upon which Michael instantly stood. "For the same reason I go every year. To do the books for Anthony Bella. Tax time. You know. I explained what I do."

"Yeah. You help people not pay their taxes."

"Is that what I said?"

Michael nodded, and climbed to the windowledge over the sink.

George put the coffeepot down on the stove.

"Mom said—"

"You want some Wheaties or Pep?"

"Pep—I should say you're a tax consultant and not an accountant."

"That's what she said?"

"I said I want Pep."

George put the Wheaties back on the shelf.

"She said if you said you're a tax consultant, you could make a fortune."

"She said that to *you*?"

"To grandma."

"Oh yeah."

"She said you were brilliant."

"*Grandma?*"

"Mom."

"Right. Brilliant." George shook his head. George could picture the conversation, undoubtedly started by Helen's mother with a line like, "Helen, why don't you buy a ———?" after some valiant face-saving efforts ("Because we don't need a ———") Helen would admit, "We can't afford a ———," her mother would counter, "Your *friends* all have a ———," and Helen would leap to George's defense.

The thing was, Helen believed that defense. She really believed that George was brilliant, and further, if he'd only Be More Aggressive, he could scratch to Olympian heights of Success. A lot of fierce and solemn energy went into Helen's Belief In George, and it left him grateful, touched . . . and exhausted. In fact, this fierce-and-solemn approach was not really characteristic of Helen, just something she'd read about in *McCall's* in an article entitled "Three Things Every Young Bride Should Do"; the other two were tuna casseroles. That George was completely aware of this fact did not leave him any less touched . . . or exhausted.

"Tax consultant," he said it out loud. "Do I want to be a 'Tax Consultant' when I grow up?"

Michael giggled. "You *are* grown-up."

George poured himself a soupbowl of Wheaties and added some chocolate sauce. "Wanna bet?"

A very peculiar thing happened in the bedroom.

George had left the radio on, and while he was dressing, Bill Tabbert sang "Younger Than Springtime" . . . and George remembered his earlier dream, a dream so pungent it seemed once again to be filling the air: He'd been lying on sand in the South Pacific, youth and joy invading his arms. Scowling slightly, George shook his head, and for just a second, the sight of his wife, peacefully resting on percale sheets, clashed against visions of red hibiscus, angel-lovers and gentle lips; and suddenly George felt a terrible pang, a nameless longing, a nameless fear. He gave it a name:

S-e-x.

In panic, he thought about waking Helen (he could ask his daughter, Debbie, to cough) but he didn't have time—a two-hour drive to Idlewild Airport, his plane departing at nine A.M.—and in any event, would it be like starlight? Warmer than music? Softer than June? Could sleeping on a Sealy Posturepedic mattress *ever* approximate sleeping on *sand*?

There were times such questions had stabbed him before, but never had the pangs been quite so intense. He considered the option of indigestion and hurriedly opened the bathroom chest, looking for—

Trojans.

A pack of Trojans winked from the shelf.

"Take me," it whispered, "take me along."

"Don't be ridiculous," George said aloud.

He'd never cheated on Helen before.

He wasn't intending to cheat on her now.

"*Youth . . . joy . . .*" the radio sang; George eyed the packet with deep dismay, as though he expected a tiny army to climb through the cardboard and conquer his fort.

"*Lips . . . June . . .*" The radio hammered, and just for a second the universe reeled, logic failed, and a tiny army of Trojan warriors marched through a bathroom in Clifton, New Jersey.

Troy conquered.

Helen slept.

DORIS

TWO

"Tony threw up, Tony threw up," Annie was chanting. "Pee-*yew*."

"*Not*," he returned with a healthy holler. "*Dog* did it. Boy are you dumb."

"Pee-*yew*," Annie retorted.

Doris put down the pastry pen and followed the noise to the door of the den.

"Pee-YEW," Annie repeated, pummeling Tony who pummeled her back. "OUCH."

"*Stop* it, darnit! you'll wake the *baby*," Doris exploded; she looked at the rug, in the center of which was a giant yuch. She looked at the ceiling and back at the rug and then back at the ceiling and back at the rug where the children were glued to a flickering set whose sound hadn't worked in a week and a half while a sick-looking spaniel under the couch lay strewn in a wreckage of chocolate crumbs.

"Who fed her cake?" Doris demanded.

Total silence.

The telephone rang.

"Somebody get me some paper towels." Doris had already moved to the phone. The children remained at the flickering set, where Tom battled Jerry with silent guns. "You both para*ple*gic?" Doris accused.

"What's para*lee*gic?" Tony inquired.

"Unable to move. . . . Oh, Christ," she pleaded and crossed herself quickly as nobody moved and the baby bellowed and her hand went down to the yammering phone.

A total stranger from Arthur Murray offered her rhumba lessons, free. Doris said she was paraplegic.

The man stammered.

Doris hung up.

"What's para*lee*gic?" Tony inquired.

"Oh, never mind. I'll get them myself." Doris went off for the paper towels, pursued by a terrible gnawing fear that she'd just enacted a piece of damage on a growing pair of incipient minds. According to "Doctor, What Should I Do?" children should never be *forced* to help but should learn it, instead, through "a chain of rewards." According to "Can This Child Be Saved?" work should *not* always be rewarded, "concepts of duty *have* to be taught," and "How Do You Rate as a Mother?" (for March) said wailing babies should never be spoiled. Kim wailed. Doris picked up the paper towels and ran to her baby.

The doorbell rang.

Doris picked up her red-faced child and held her tenderly, rubbing her back, kissing the soft fuzz of her hair. Kim howled.

The doorbell rang.

Holding both Kim and the paper towels, she ran to the hallway. "Coming," she yelled, as Kim let go of some earlier carrots, and paper toweling rolled to the floor.

Liz McLaughlin stood on the landing, sunlight glinting her auburn hair, a rather hot-and-harried expression smearing her smooth, sardonic face. Liz wore a new Anne Fogarty dress, with a bell-shaped crinoline, spike-heeled shoes, seamless stockings, snakeskin bag, and fingertips shiny with Fire and Ice. Liz was the best-dressed woman in town, though the town, being Oakland, did not much care.

"Sorry I'm late," she swept through the door. "The traffic tonight was completely insane. Wuzzamatter, baby?" she crooned at Kim, who yowled. "So the guy didn't call you again. You can't keep on going to pieces like this."

"Cute," Doris said. "Cute." She grimaced.

Liz had stooped to recover the towels. "So? What's new?"

"Oh . . . not a lot. There's something really rotten on the rug and Kim doesn't care for my Gerber's carrots."

"So I see." Liz was squinting from Doris's shoulder to the ripe, disheartening view of the rug. "I knew there was a reason I never got married. I'll take the baby, you take the rug."

They met in the kitchen a few minutes later. Doris had changed to a terry cloth robe. Liz had already heated the coffee.

"I bet you'll be glad to get out of this mess. Now tell me—honestly. Where are you going?"

"I *told* you honestly," Doris complained. She picked up the Home-Baker's Pastree Pen and menaced it over the frosted cake. "I'm going—honestly—on a retreat."

"With nuns and fathers."

"Fathers and nuns. They don't *bother* you," Doris looked up. "They just kind of leave you alone to think."

"You can *think,* dear heart, at the Fairmont Hotel." Liz poured some cream. "And the food's better."

"You don't understand. . . . God-double-dammit will you look what I *did*?" Doris looked down at the lopsided cake, which said, in pink, against yellow goo:

HAPPY BIRTHDAY

Liz giggled. "Well . . . I guess they'll get the idea. Who's birthday?"

"Harry's mother."

"Have some coffee."

"If I sit, I'll collapse."

"Okay. Collapse." Frowning, Liz poured a cup of coffee and pushed it at Doris. "I said—collapse."

Doris collapsed. A long and truly terrible sigh started to worm its way through her lips.

"Okay," Liz said, "now I told you I'd take the dog for the weekend and sit with kids until Harry gets home, but there's no law that says I can't begin now. Why don't you go take a bath or something?"

"I haven't packed."

"I'll pack for you."

Splashing around in the bubbling tub, Doris wondered what Liz would pack, what Tony would break, what Harry would eat, what his mother would say to be utterly bitchy, and whether she really should cancel her trip.

She knew that she shouldn't cancel her trip when she found herself trying to clean up the bathtub while she was in it, scattering Ajax onto her thigh.

She closed her eyes. Moments passed; silent, long, blissful, sweet.

"Hey, don't fall asleep in there, huh?"

"I'm not," Doris yawned. "What time is it now?"

"Quarter of six."

"Oh, Lord. They stop serving dinner at seven." Doris sighed and dripped to the mat and moaned as she looked at herself in the mirror. Seven pounds. She really had to lose seven pounds. She'd fast this weekend, that's what she'd do.

"You better get going," Liz hollered in. "Where is this papal flophouse, anyway?"

Doris wrapped herself up in a towel and started brushing her short black hair. "You know where the Bella Winery is? It's right around there." She entered the bedroom, powdered and dry. Liz had apparently finished the bag and was sprawled on the bed with a lit cigarette. Doris scrounged through the underwear drawer, adding, "Papal flophouse, indeed. As though your name weren't Lizzie McLaughlin."

"Oh . . . Well . . ." Liz blew a perfect circle of smoke. "It's not that I don't believe in the Pope, it's just when it really gets down to the crunch, I believe a lot more in Margaret Sanger."

"Who's Margaret Sanger?"

"Godsake, Doris. The lady who invented not having babies. The diaphragm, Doris."

"Oh. That." Thoughtfully, Doris crossed to the

closet, selecting a white, nylon blouse and a pale, blue, gabardine suit. Turning, she said, "Liz? I probably shouldn't say this . . . but I think you probably shouldn't say that."

Liz looked up. "Shouldn't say what?"

"Well . . . smarty things like that Sanger line. I mean, it's all right to say them to me—I mean, because that's what friends are *for*, but well—you know—men don't like girls to be too—"

"*Smart*?? Oh, God. You sound like my mother." Liz shook her head. "I was probably the only kid in our high school who had to skulk home when I got an A."

"Well, that's *not* what I mean. What I mean is, sometimes you're just too—"

"*Funny*??—That was the other thing, Doris. My mother used to say, 'Do you want to grow up to be Eve Arden? Always gets the laugh but never the man?' "

"I *meant*," Doris said, and reached for her hat, "you don't have to *flaunt* that you're not a virgin."

Liz nodded. "Doris, sit down."

"Why?"

"Sit down."

"Why?"

"I'm a virgin."

Doris sat down. Her mouth was a small, plum-colored *O*.

"Listen, I never *lied* to you, Doris. I just—well I just kind of let you *assume*. And the thing is that *everyone* seems to assume—just because a girl's a career woman, they—"

"What about *Bill?* I mean, you went on *vacation* with Bill."

"I didn't. I chickened out and stayed home and sat under a sunlamp."

"Oh. My God. And you brought that little grass skirt for Annie."

"Woolworth's. They had a Hawaaian Week."

"Oh."

"The truth is, Doris—I'm scared."

"Oh. Well, it isn't *scary* at all. It's just . . . kind of

boring is really what it is. I mean after you do it you say, 'This is *it*?' "

"That's what I'm scared of." Liz looked away.

Ker-*boom*! A terrible crashing sound came through the window. Doris looked out. The sky was suddenly coffee-colored; sheets of raindrops started to fall. "Oh, Lord. I better get going," she said. "When Harry gets home, will you run him a bath? I mean if he's wet? Harry gets really *terrible* colds."

"Don't worry," Liz said.

"And Kim—if she cries will you please pick her up? I decided *The Ladies' Home Journal* was wrong."

"Don't worry," Liz said.

"And Annie, she better get dressed in a dress because Harry's mother—"

"Don't *worry*," Liz said. "Have a wonderful time." She picked up the suitcase and walked to the hall, where the children's voices were bellowing:

"Dumb! Boy, are you dumb!"

"I'm gonna tell Mommy."

"Tell 'er you're dumb."

"Ouch!"

"*Ouch!!*"

"Liz . . .?" Doris said as she walked through the door. She turned. "Does Bill really love you?"

"I guess."

"Then marry him, Lizzie," she said with feeling. "Family life is a wonderful thing."

"Ker-*boom*!" said the sky.

"Dumb!" Tony yelled.

And Doris made a running dash for the car.

THE
SEA SHADOWS INN

THREE

"Well, it stopped raining." Margaret Chalmers turned from the window and looked through the small, comfortable lobby to the desk where her husband, Angus, sat. She examined them both (the desk and the husband) with a certain air of contented pride.

The desk she'd acquired the week before at a special auction in San Francisco—a sturdy, turn-of-the-century oak, which Angus had told her was "too modern" to belong in the 1840s inn. Margaret had said, by the same logic, Angus himself would be "too modern," having been born in the same era, and not being half as sturdy, at that. Angus had narrowed his hazel eyes, thrown back his giant head and laughed.

Margaret had gotten her sturdy desk; and Angus was sitting there reading the news.

He'd started wearing his bifocals now; he'd cursed, refused them for almost a year, swearing, "I can't abide 'em, Maggie. Damn things make me dizzy and *sick*."

"You're just not used to them," Margaret had said.

"I'm not used to being *fifty*," he'd countered. "*That's* what I can't get *used* to, Maggie."

"Well . . ." she'd smiled at him, "better try."

"Yeah? The hell with it," Angus had groused. "By the time I got used to being fifty, damned if I wouldn't be fifty-one."

Angus was practically fifty-one. A tall, narrow, angular man with a tall, narrow, angular face. His hair had once been autumnal red, but now it was showing the signs of winter. Handsome, a very handsome man, Margaret concluded, and poked at the fire.

Angus was laughing. "Listen to this. They're gonna investigate Ingrid Bergman."

"Who is?" Margaret sat on the couch.

"Congress, Maggie. Congress is who. This congressman fella. Listen to this: 'Her shocking extra-marital affair threatens the structure of American life. In fact, it's downright un-American.' So somebody tells him she *isn't* American—listen to this—so he thinks it over and says, 'Thank God.' " Angus roared.

Margaret frowned. "How old is that paper?"

"Hell, I dunno. It was lining the drawer." Angus looked at the top of the page. "Well it's a year ago. What the hell. The point I'm making is all the same. Whole generation's a damn buncha prudes." Angus stretched, and lit up a smoke. "I tell you, Maggie, give me the twenties. At least we knew how to have fun back then." He gave her his grin. "Didn't we, kid."

She smiled at him, flushing, and looked at the fire, remembering a night back in '29, a sawdust speakeasy over a barn, where she and Angus had met and—

"Hi!"

Angus looked up.

A nice-looking fellow came through the door, his coat-collar up, an overnight suitcase under his arm. Frowning, Angus removed his glasses. "Oh. Mr. Peters." Angus stood, and walked to the counter. "Good to see you. Well, no thanks to these goddamn glasses. Hell, you know—you gotta look *up* or you can't see *far*."

Clearly, Peters didn't know. He'd cocked his head with a kind of politely impatient smile. "Well," Angus said, clearing his throat, "I suppose you want cottage seven again."

"That'd be fine." Peters yawned, and looked at his watch. "You still serving dinner?"

"Yeah. Sure. Till nine thirty. You made it with twenty minutes to spare. . . . How long does it take to fly here anyway?"

"Well, not counting the difference in time"—Peters

looked at his watch again—"thirteen hours, twenty-two minutes, and fourteen seconds."

"That's pretty fast."

"Not for a passenger."

Angus laughed. "You just want to hurry in there and eat, I could take your bag to the cottage."

"Oh. Swell. Thanks, Mr. Chalmers. That'd be great." Peters stopped at the magazine rack and picked up a *Saturday Evening Post*. "Dinner partner," he grinned at Margaret, who smiled and watched him leaving the room.

"Nice," she reflected, after he'd gone. "He always seems such a nice young man . . . I think he looks a little like Larry, don't you?"

"Sure," Angus said. "Around the toes. Dammit, Maggie. Every time a kid walks in here with dark brown hair he 'looks a little like Larry' to you. Honey—" he suddenly softened his voice—"if we'd sent him away to college or something, we wouldn't have seen him for six months, either."

"South Korea is not college."

"Neither was Flanders and I came back."

"One thing has nothing to do with the other. Besides—I didn't know you in World War One, so I didn't have to worry."

"Maggie, Maggie." Angus put Peters's bag on the floor and crossed to the couch. He looked at his wife. Her beauty was starting to blur a little, but he'd found that he found the lines around her eyes supremely touching. "Honey, we're all gonna live to a thousand. We're all gonna live to be disgustingly decrepit. Larry will live to wear bifocals, too."

She laughed at him then, and Angus kissed her.

"Chees it," she muttered. "Somebody's coming!"

"Prude," said Angus, pulling away.

Doris was lost. . . . Or rather, Route 29 was lost. It had wandered away at an intersection, and absolutely never come back. Doris had looked. She'd asked for directions. People gave them, rapidly reeling off Rights and Lefts. Doris had listened, bright and attentive, nodding politely, smiling thanks, and then driven off completely confused, remembering only the first instruction—"Left at the corner." Or was it Right? Doris was nearly ready to scream.

The trouble had started at seven o'clock when Jimmy Fidler reported the news: "*Romance at last has come to*—" and the radio suddenly burst into static, which left her wondering, come to *who*? She'd really racked her brains for a while (Farley Granger? Debbie Reynolds?) and then she'd suddenly started to laugh. What, after all, did it matter to *her*? And further, really, what was romance? It had something to do with Whitman Samplers, huge diamonds, Gregory Peck, and the Jon Whitcomb girls with the stars in their eyes—but what did *that* have to do with *life*? Hers, for instance. She tried to think.

Absolutely nothing came to her mind.

Doris sighed.

Static continued filling the air. *Sssssssshhhhh.*

She tried to pursue the thought.

When she'd first met Harry, what had she felt?

She tried to remember six years back to the age of eighteen, to a basketball game in her senior year, when Rosalind Baker's brother Harry had come to the game with his uniform on. All the girls had been conscious of Harry, who looked very strong and tremendously tough. But Doris had dinner at Rosalind's later, and found he was sweet and tremendously shy.

She'd found him . . . touching.

Later, she'd found him touching her breast, and that was nice.

And that was that.

The static had very suddenly died. Doris had found herself totally lost. Now, it was several hours later, and Doris was facing a neon sign:

SEA SHADOWS INN

She made the turn, parking her car in the front of the lot. She needed a map. She needed advice. She desperately needed a ladies' room now. And a rest. And a Coke. And a cup of coffee and a chocolate sundae with marshmallow sauce.

Which she woudn't eat.

She was going to fast.

The trouble with a fast, Doris reflected, as she walked to the porch of the Sea Shadows Inn, was simply that it wasn't fast. It was slow. Terribly, meanly, miserably slow. Every hour passed like a decade. A minute encompassed the Irish Famine; fifteen minutes included the life of Mahatma Ghandi and the first seven weeks at the Donner Pass; a half an hour . . .

Doris shuddered. She opened the door and entered the lobby and stood for a moment, looking around. The lobby was charming and very . . . romantic. The word just popped to the top of her head. There were chintz curtains on leaded windows, a pale green carpet and warm-looking wood, and off to the side, in a kind of a nook, a pair of love seats covered in chintz; a fireplace glowed.

Romantic. The word insisted itself.

She made a surprisingly wistful sigh, heard it, frowned, and walked to the desk. A gnarly-looking proprietor smiled, cocked his head, and thumbed at his right. "There," he told her.

Doris turned, found herself facing a Powder Room door, and wondered how the man could tell what she wanted. A few minutes later, in front of the mirror, she saw it was terribly easy to tell. A person could take one look at her and tell: here's a respectable married woman who should lose seven pounds and will not want a meal; also a woman who will not want a room, since she hasn't any luggage or a Dangerous Look, which left her as a woman who could only want a Powder Room.

Doris was now completely depressed.

George hand finished his shrimp cocktail, including the lettuce. He looked around. He was all alone. There was nobody else in the dining room now. He chewed his parsley and heard himself chew. He opened his *Saturday Evening Post*. Behind its Norman Rockwell cover it offered a piece on the Red Menace, Congressman Nixon, and several stories. "Never a case of throat irritation from smoking Camels," Dick Powell said. "They agree with my throat." George turned the page. Nash had a winner for '51. La Motta was favored to win next week. A fabulous Orange Kiss-Me Cake had won in the Pillsbury National Bake-Off. Pepsodent gave you a winning smile. The world, it seemed was loaded with winners. George lit a Camel and thought about that. He checked his watch; it was getting late. He looked for the waiter, a very old man who was nowhere in sight. He drummed the table, and looked at the woman who stood, alone, at the dining room door, looking uncertain and biting her lip.

She was nice to look at, and something about her was making him smile. Chalmers came up and asked her something. The woman seemed to be giving it thought. She thought for a while and nodded yes. Chalmers led her off to a corner table.

George continued drumming on his, watching the woman taking a seat, taking a menu, taking a look.

He looked at the woman.

She looked away.

The woman looked up.

George looked away.

He looked at the window.

He looked at the door.

He looked at the woman.

She looked at the floor.

"Sir?" He looked at the ancient waiter, the giant platter, the sizzling steak.

"Thank you, Albert," he said politely, and turned his attention back to his plate. He salted his meat, mashed his potatoes, salted his salad; he ate for a while. Then, very slowly, and very coolly, as though it were something he did every day, George looked up.

The woman looked down.
She looked at her menu.

"Coffee," she said to the hovering waiter. "Bring me some coffee. *Just* coffee." She paused for a moment. "While I decide." The waiter nodded, moving away.

The question remained; what should she eat, *if* she should eat, which she hadn't decided, but *if* she should eat, she should certainly order a broiled steak, except that the steak was seven-fifty.

She checked her wallet, which highly recommended spaghetti.

Doris sighed, and looked at her waist.

She looked at the man.

The man looked away.

George was looking at Albert now. Albert was sourly writing her check. Clearly, all the woman could afford was the coffee, which made her a genuine Dame In Distress, and George got a sudden flicker of himself, in white armor on a shining horse, swimming the mountain, slaying the moat, and placing his jacket over the dragon. He beckoned the waiter.

"Steak for the lady."

"Steak?" said the waiter.

"Medium rare. With all the trimmings." George liked himself.

He looked at the lady.

The lady was watching her sugar bowl now. She picked it up; she put it down; she picked it up.

There was nothing in that. George looked back at his food and ate. Four bites of meat, three of potato, and half a mouthful of salad later, he casually moved his eyes to the right. The girl was busy protesting the steak. Albert shrugged and pointed at George, who lifted a forkful by way of a toast.

The girl giggled.

George smiled.

* * *

"Gee, that was awfully nice of you," she said, as George joined her. "You shouldn't have. Really."

"Yeah. But you're awfully glad that I did. You must've been hungry." He looked at the plate. "You ate everything on it except the design."

Flushing a little, she checked the design. "I think I nibbled a few nasturtiums and maybe a tiny wing from the bird." She tilted her head. "You think they'll arrest me?"

"Not if we're clever. We'll tell them we saw the bird eat the flower and then clip his wing on a low-hanging branch. They can give me the third degree for a week, but I'm iron, baby. I'll never crack."

The girl giggled. "I'm Doris Baker."

"George Peters," George said, and then couldn't think of a thing to add. "Sugar?"

"Now, look—" the girl said abruptly—"I'm a married woman and I don't—"

"For your coffee."

"Oh."

"And I'm also a married man."

"Yes. I know. I noticed the ring."

"I know. I noticed you notice the ring. Thanks."

"For what?"

"For noticing the ring. I mean, it was kind of a compliment."

"Oh. Well I didn't *mean* it as a compliment."

"Oh."

"Oh dear. Well, I didn't mean *that* as an insult. What I mean is, I guess I meant it as a compliment."

"Thanks."

"You're welcome."

George looked around. He waved for the waiter. "Coffee and brandy," he said, "in the den." He shrugged at the girl. "Well, why not?" The girl looked nervous. He found himself happy the girl looked nervous. It had been a long time since he'd made a girl nervous.

It made him nervous.

He bumped his knee getting up from the table.

* * *

"How about bed?" Angus said. "It's after midnight."

Margaret smiled.

"Look at them, Angus. Don't they look nice?" She was pointing at the girl and the Peters fellow, sitting on the love seat, next to the fire.

"Well, I bet they're gonna look rotten tomorrow. I think they've had about seven stingers."

"I remember when *we* could have seven stingers and not look rotten."

"How about bed?" Angus repeated. "It's after midnight."

Margaret smiled.

"So *then*," George was saying, "we landed at Normandy, an' I was the pointman, you know what I mean?"

"No," Doris said. "What do you mean?"

"Means you're the first one into the pool."

"You were the *leader*?"

"Nah. Just the first. The first target. You walk into range, you're the first one they shoot. So the point about being the pointman is, after you're dead, the next guy can figure out where not to walk." George laughed. He was feeling no pain.

"Gee," she told him. "You must've been brave."

"Yeah. Sure. Brave. I pissed."

"What?"

"I pissed." He suddenly winced. "Boy, I really just *told* you that. You know . . . I never told *anyone* that? I mean, nobody, ever . . . not even my *wife*? Gee . . ." He looked at her. "Gee," he repeated. "You're very easy to talk to, Dorothy. Wow. I really feel close to you."

"Mmm. You are . . ." She suddenly bolted upright. "I think you're a little bit *too* close, George. I mean, I think you should move away." George moved away. "But not that far."

He moved back quickly; he put his arm back around her shoulder. Doris sighed. She was very high. She knew she was high. She didn't care. On the other hand, she *cared* that she didn't care. But then somehow, she didn't care that she cared. She was very confused. She was very relaxed. She was terribly tense. There were tiny tingles exploring her spine; there was somebody jumping around in her stomach. Closing her eyes, she could see who it was—a trio of cheerleaders, waving pom-poms, hollering "Yay!" and Doris could make out the single letter written on each of their burgeoning chests:

S-

E-

Doris stood up. "I really have to go," she said very quickly.

George said nothing. His stomach churned; his arm felt suddenly empty now. He looked at her. God, she was really cute. She was darling, adorable, wonderful, sweet, and George felt a sudden surge of warmth, a terrible tropical-island heat. There was sand in his shoes; he smelled hibiscus. Somewhere, faintly, a radio played, and the tune it was playing went round in his head. "You don't really *have* to go," he said hoarsely, then hearing his hoarseness, he said, "You have to. Listen, you really *have* to go."

"I know," she nodded.

"I'll walk you," he said.

She nodded again. She straightened her skirt and the seams of her stockings; she reached for her hat, her bag, and her gloves.

They walked through the totally empty lobby. Doris could feel her heart really pound. God, he was handsome, not really handsome, just kind of *handsome* is what he was, and very romantic; the way he looked at her now was romantic; oh, she would have to go to confession; he *was* handsome (Bless me, Father); he'd made her laugh (for I have sinned).

"No, I haven't," she said out loud. They stood at her car.

"Haven't what?"

She opened the door. "Nothing," she answered.

"Yeah. I know. I haven't either."

"Well . . ." she said, and reached for her keys. "Well . . ." she repeated. "Good night, George."

He nodded slowly. "Good night."

"Well . . . good night," she said.

"Good night."

"I have to go."

"I know. Good night."

"Good night."

"Do you really *have* to go?"

She nodded. "I really have to go."

"I know."

"Good night. . . . You better get off the running board, George."

"I know. Good night."

"I know."

"Good night."

FOUR

It was warm and sunny in California, but George was dreaming of heavy snow. Pure, clean, virginal snow; white as percale; Rinso White.

George awakened, slightly dazed, yawned widely, and noticed a lady's hand on his chest. It was not Helen's. For a long moment he focused on the hand that was not Helen's. It had five fingers, just like Helen's, an opposable thumb, just like Helen's, a plain gold band, just like Helen's; it was not Helen's. Very, very, very slowly, Goerge moved his eyes to the side of the bed:

It was not Helen's.

"Jesus Christ!" He leapt to his feet, saw he was naked, and covered his mouth. Behind it, he very silently screamed. Scattered around on the yellow rug was a girdle-bra-pants-slip-shorts-socks-stockings-shirt-blouse-tie-belt-slacks-skirt-jacket-belt-bag-scarf-jacket-coat-hat-coat-hat-shoes-shoes-gloves.

George finished screaming and let out a groan. Cajoling his fingers out of his mouth, he picked up a sock and examined it closely to be sure it was his, because if it wasn't, things might not really be as bad as they looked.

The sock fit.

George put it on.

Steeling himself, he looked at the bed. The girl was lying curled on her side, her hair falling softly around her cheek. She looked adorable. George panicked. He put on his jacket and frantically started combing his hair.

"Hey that's a sharp-looking outfit," she said.

George whirled around. "Um," he said. "Hi!" he added.

He looked at her quickly, straight in the eye. Her eyes were very wide. And blue. And scared. Or maybe she wasn't scared.

"What time is it?" she said.

She wasn't scared. A girl who could blithely ask for the time at a time like this was not scared.

"I don't know. My watch is next to the bed."

Holding the sheet up under her chin, she slowly groped at the bedside table. George very quickly put on his pants.

"It's *three o'clock*?"

He turned around quickly with a shoe in his hand. "No. It's twenty-five after eight. The stem's broken. It's six hours and thirty-five minutes fast. At home, it's *three* hours and thirty-five minutes fast. The stem's broken," he explained again.

"Oh." She reached for her petticoat now and, under the covers, wriggled it on. He looked at her slowly. She looked very cheerful and Terribly Bright. "Why don't you get it fixed?" she said.

He shrugged. "I don't know. I was going to, but then I got used to it."

"Oh . . . but doesn't it—doesn't it mix you up?"

"No . . . I'm very clever with figures." He looked at hers, swathed in covers, remembered what it looked like without the covers, and panicked again. He started to pace, one shoe on, one in his hand. He stopped pacing, let out a moan, leaned on the dresser and glared at her now.

"Why are you looking at me like that?"

"Why do you have to look so . . . *luminous*?" George accused.

"*What?*"

He started pacing again. "I mean, it would make everything so much easier if you woke up with puffy eyes and blotchy skin like everyone else."

She smiled, shrugging. "God figured chubby thighs was enough."

He pictured her thighs.

Oh God.

He wheeled. "Will you just stop *joking*?" he exploded. "This is *terribly serious*!"

"Oh." She nodded, holding the faintly stupid smile. Maybe she was stupid, he hoped wildly. *That* would help. He looked at her. No, that wouldn't help. "Look," he said firmly, "Look, this is *not* gonna just go away. We've *got* to discuss it."

"Sure. Okay." She got out of bed, pulled out the blanket, wrapped it around her, and walked to the door.

"Where are you *going*?"

"I thought—I thought I'd just brush my teeth . . . first," she added.

"Dorothy . . . sit down," George commanded.

She opened her mouth.

"Dorothy—sit!"

She sat—with the blanket still wrapped around her—on the edge of one of the chintz-covered chairs. George felt better as soon as she sat. More in control. Now all he had to find was the words. Something nice and kind . . . and final. He paced the cottage, carefully keeping his eyes from the bed. He walked as far as the leaded window. "*Life is like a window*," he thought about saying, "*and the thing is, I have to look out for myself.*" No, he decided. Much too harsh. He paced to the piano. "*True, we made beautiful music together—*" Yuch! The words would stick in his throat. Fireplace. Fire! There had to be something. "*Listen, we started a fire—*"

She cleared her throat.

George turned around. "Listen," he said, grimly, sincerely. "Dorothy, first of all . . . I want you to know that last night was the most beautiful, fantastic, wonderful, crazy thing that's ever happened to me and I'll never forget it—or you."

Perfect.

"Doris," she said abruptly.

"What?"

"Doris. My name's Doris."

"Your name's *Doris?*" George sat down. "I've been calling you Dorothy all night long. Why the hell didn't you tell me before?"

"Well . . . I didn't expect us to end up . . . you know . . . and then when I *did* try to tell you . . . you weren't listening."

"When?" he pursued, noticed his fly was open and zipped it.

"Well, it was . . . you know . . . in the middle of . . . things."

"Oh." He looked at her, picturing Things. "Jesus, that was *incredible*, wasn't it? Really *incredible*."

"It was . . . nice."

He cocked his head.

"Especially the last time," she added quickly.

He winced. "I know—I'm an animal! Jesus!" George threw his second shoe at the wall, and paced, berating himself, to the window. Christ, if Kinsey had interviewed *him*—"I don't know—I don't know what got *into* me," he said. "I just—" He frowned, and suddenly turned. "What was the matter with the first two times?"

"Hmmm?" She was busy gathering clothes. She gave his question serious thought. "Well. The first time was kind of fast, and the second—" she stopped. "You really want to *hear* this? I mean, I feel funny talking about it."

"It was very, very beautiful, Doris. There was nothing dirty or disgusting in what we did."

She nodded slowly, watching his face. "Then how come you look so down in the dumps?"

He nodded slowly. "Because my wife's gonna *kill* me, Doris."

"Don't be ridiculous. How would she know?"

"She knows already."

"How could she know? I thought you said she was home in New Jersey, My God, you didn't *call* her in the middle of the night?"

"Of course I didn't *call* her in the middle of the night.

It doesn't matter. She knows. She's the Lamont Cranston of Clifton, New Jersey."

"What?"

"Look. I don't want to talk about it now. I really think we should talk about us. There are things we have to get settled, Doris." He looked at her levelly. "Was it really as incredible for you as for me?"

She tilted her head. "Do all men like to talk about it afterwards?"

"How would *I* know if all men like to talk about it afterwards." *Did* all men like to talk about it afterwards? George didn't know. "Why?" he said suddenly. "You think I'm some kind of a pervert or something?"

"No. I just wondered." She picked up her blouse. He started to wonder. He scraped his mind, looking for the comfort of a Kinsey Statistic. "Ninety-seven point seven percent of all men like to talk about it afterwards." That would be reassuringly nice. Not that it mattered. He put on his shirt and watched as she carefully buttoned her blouse. And what about her? Maybe she'd been with nine-hundred guys and so far they'd all talked about it afterwards. Maybe she was taking a goddam poll. For Kinsey. He picked up his tie and got mad.

"The reason I asked," she was zipping her skirt, "is for information. I mean, well—you see—I was a virgin when I got married. At least . . . sort of."

He felt relieved. Sort of. "What do you mean, 'sort of'?"

"Well, I was pregnant. But I don't count that."

He closed an eye. "Doris, that counts."

"Well, I mean, by the man I married."

"Oh. I'm sorry."

"Oh. That's okay." She sat on the bed now and put on her stockings. "See, Harry and me would've gotten married anyway. It just kind of speeded things up a bit." She laughed. "Turns out I get pregnant if we drink from the same cup."

"Oh God."

"What's the matter?"

"Nothing. Never mind. Trojans are very reliable."

"Who?"

"Just—never mind." He watched her as she finished hooking her stockings. It was fascinating. He moaned. "Oh God. I'm in terrible trouble."

"Huh?" She looked up with her big blue eyes.

"I think I love you."

"Oh." She looked down. "I really better brush my teeth now," she said. She checked his eyes. "Okay?"

"Okay."

She nodded, got up, and walked to the bathroom. Without even thinking, he followed her in. She took his Ipana from the edge of the sink, squeezed it on her finger and rubbed at her teeth. It was fascinating.

"Crazy," he said. "This is really crazy!" He started to pace; he paced to the wall. Groaning, he sat on the edge of the tub. "I mean, I don't know anything about you. I don't even know—I don't even know if you like *Catcher in the Rye.*"

"*Who?*" She looked up with her finger in her mouth.

"Well you see—I have this test for people. If they don't like *Catcher in the Rye* and *Death of a Salesman,* I know right away that I won't like *them.*"

"I never even finished high school."

"You see?"

She was rinsing her mouth out. Fascinating.

"You see?" he moaned. "I don't even *care.* And I'm really a snob about education." He shook his head slowly. "Oh boy. Oh boy. I should've known something like this would happen. When it comes to love, I've got a brown thumb. Nothing goes right. Ever."

She frowned. "What do you mean?"

"Okay, listen. I'll tell you what I mean. The first time I had sex, I was eighteen years old. We were in the back seat of a parked 1938 Dodge sedan. Right in the middle, we were rear-ended."

"Oh," she sympathized. "That's really awful. . . . Did you have insurance?"

"And take last night—" George looked up. She was leaning over him. "What's the matter?"

"Nothing. I just want to turn on the water. Of the bathtub?"

"Oh." He slid further down on the edge of the tub. "Where was I?"

"Last night."

"Oh yeah. Last night. That's a perfect example. You know what the radio was playing last night while we made love?"

She apparently didn't.

"If I Knew You Were Coming, I'd Have Baked A Cake"!

She narrowed her eyes. "So?"

"*So?* So that's what's going to be 'our song.' I mean, other people would get 'Be My Love,' or 'Some Enchanted Evening.' Me? I get 'If I Knew You Were Coming I'd Have Baked A Cake.' " He rested his case.

She suddenly smiled. "You really *are* romantic, aren't you? I really like that."

He smiled back. "And what about you?"

"Gee—I don't know."

"Well, what do you think?"

"I think—I think you better go now, George."

"Go?"

"So I can get into the tub. You know . . . take a bath?"

He looked at the tub, and made the connection. He looked at Doris. "You're all dressed. You got all dressed up to get into the bathtub?"

"No. I just *decided* I want to take a bath."

He looked at her slowly with the corner of his eye. "Doris, you don't feel dirty, do you?"

"No. I don't feel dirty, George. I just want—"

"Because what we did, wasn't dirty, Doris."

"I know, George, I simply want to take a bath."

"Honestly?"

"Yes. Honestly, George."

"Okay. . . ." He hovered in the doorway for a minute. "Okay," he repeated, and walked through the door. He walked back in.

"What?" she said.

"Nothing. I just want to say . . . good-bye."

"Good-bye?"

"I mean . . . good-bye until after your bath."

"Oh . . ." She gave him a gorgeous grin. "Oh, George . . ."

"Oh, Doris . . ." He smiled. "Oh shit!" he added and walked through the door, but he left smiling.

Still smiling, she closed the door.

Alone in the bedroom, George was suffused with a new wave of guilt.

He made the bed. He lay on it. He kicked off his shoes, and looked at his watch, and stared, a little numbly, at the beamed ceiling.

Only twenty-six hours ago, he'd been standing in front of his own sink, mentally wrestling a package of condoms, and the only reason he'd allowed them to win, was simply because he was totally sure he was too unlucky to get to use them. And his notion of "luck," at that innocent hour, was not *remotely* Doris Baker. It was Dagmar. George knew Dagmar was a tacky fantasy, but there you had it. George had a tacky fantasy-life. All he'd dreamt in his wildest dreams was a nightful of totally meaningless sex with a giant dumb, big-breasted

Alone in the bathroom, Doris was suddenly gripped with guilt. It gripped her throat.

She wanted to scream. Very methodically, she reached for the big, fluffy towel, wadded it into her mouth, and screamed. She felt better. She closed her eyes. Lord. Only fourteen hours ago, she'd been splashing around in her own tub, and planning on nothing worse than a fast. She sighed. Where had she gone wrong? She nodded: When she'd gone off Route 29. Route 29 was clearly the Straight-And-Narrow Path. God spoke in parables, strange and obtuse. The devil spoke with Jimmy Fidler's voice. If it hadn't been for him and his damned report about Hollywood romance—*"The fault is in our stars, not in ourselves . . ."* That was a quote from something, and she didn't blonde. And God, In His Infinite Sense Of Humor, had sent him a small, rounded brunette. That was bad enough. But why, he questioned the beamed ceiling, why did it have to be a *meaningful* brunette?

And further, what did meaningful *mean*?

He loved Helen. He really did.

So how could he possibly love someone else? And someone as thoroughly different from Helen? Because she was thoroughly different from Helen. That's why. Doris had freckles; Helen had none. But it wasn't just that. Doris had freckles on her personality. That was it. She was imperfect. Maybe as imperfect as George himself. And that was so . . . invigorating.

The telephone rang. George leapt up as though he'd been shot. He eyed the instrument with total panic. It was Helen all right. Because Helen *knew*. He knew she knew.

It rang again. Heart pounding, George picked it up, and then with a sudden burst of inspiration, picked it up with a Slavic accent.

"Ullo," he intoned.

know what. Sometimes she felt tremendously stupid. And wicked. She'd once gone to confession because she had a dream about Cary Grant. The priest had been funny. He'd said, Okay, now dream about six Hail Marys. This time it wasn't funny. She soaped herself with a cake of Ivory. Up till today, she'd been pure as Ivory. Ninety-nine and forty-four one-hundreths percent.

She loved Harry. She really did.

And George was crazy. Completely nuts. He never stopped talking. And half of what he said was so . . . silly. And that was it. Exactly what she found so endearing about him. He was kind of like a—well, vacation from Reality. George was goofy. Maybe as goofy as Doris herself. And that was so . . . she couldn't find the word . . .

Comforting?

No. It was just . . . fun.

Her heart pounded. She leapt from the bathtub as though she'd been shot. She had to get dressed. She had to get dressed and go very quickly to Saint Bartholomew's. God *knew*.

"Oh God," she thought,

"George?"

He sighed. It was Tony Bella.

"Tony," he said. "Thank God."

"Huh?"

"Nothing." He sat up in bed. "What's up?"

"Nothing. Just wanted to make sure *you* were. We've got a date for a quarter of nine."

"Right. I'll meet you at the office."

"Right."

George hung up. The world was a normal place after all. With normal meetings at a quarter of nine. And not only that, George was hungry. He would be all right. A hungry man was a well man. He picked up the phone, in a moment he would later live to regret, and ordered a huge, wonderful breakfast. He hung up the phone, lit a cigarette, and thought compulsively of eggs and bacon, Wheaties and toast.

He was already cured.

Things would be fine.

and then decided to stop thinking.

Doris made her mind a total blank:

She came out of the bathroom, totally dressed, except she was barefoot, and holding a girdle and stockings in her hand. She tossed them on the bed.

"We have to talk," he said grimly. He was sitting on the upright piano now, with his feet on the bench. "Things have changed. I'm not in love with you any more." He paused. "I'm *desperately* in love with you, Doris." He jumped to the floor. "And now you want to hear something even *worse*?—I'm *happily* married."

She cocked her head. "George, are you Jewish?"

"No, I'm not Jewish. As a matter of fact, I'm Methodist. Why?"

"Oh. Are Methodists big on guilt?" She crossed to the dressing table off at the right.

He stared at her. "Christ, don't *you* feel guilty?"

She turned. "Oh boy, are you *kidding*?" she said. "Half my high school class became nuns."

"Oh yeah?" He paced to the fireplace again, and started placing the logs for a fire. "Catholics have rules about this kind of thing."

"Yeah. We've got rules about everything," she said, pulling a makeup kit from her bag. "That's what's so great about being Catholic. You know where you stand."

"Yeah, well I know where I stand, too. I'm standing in the seventh circle of Hell." He lit the fire.

"You Italian?" she asked.

"Hey, what's with you and nationalities?"

"Well, I just wondered. You're so *emotional*." She powdered her nose.

"I happen," he said with great dignity, "I happen to be a C.P.A."

"What's that supposed to mean?"

"I mean I can be as logical as the next person."

"Oh. That's funny." She watched him in the mirror. "I mean, you don't seem the accountant type."

"Well, I'm *not* the accountant type. That's why I'm an accountant."

She squinted in the mirror.

"It's simple," he explained. "My whole life has always been a terrible mess. Figures always come out nice and tidy, right on the button. What are you?"

"Italian."

He frowned. "Then how come you aren't *more* emotional?"

"It's simple," she explained. "When you grow up

with a large Italian family, it's enough to turn you off emotionally for life."

He sat on the bed. "I wondered why you weren't crying or yelling or anything."

"I was. Before. I did it in the bathroom."

"I didn't hear you."

"I know. I stuffed a towel in my mouth."

"Oh. I'm sorry."

"That's okay." She finished her lips and put away the lipstick. "No use crying over spilt milk."

"You're right!" He was trying to match her lightness.

She closed her bag with a competent snap. "Then how come we're feeling so lousy," she moaned.

"Because," he said, nodding somberly, "we're two decent, honest people and what we've done is tearing us apart. I mean, I know it wasn't our fault, but I keep on seeing the faces of my children and the look of betrayal in their sweet little eyes. I keep thinking of our marriage vows, the trust my wife has placed in me, the experiences we've shared together. And you know what the worse part of it is? Right this minute, while I'm thinking all this, I have this fantastic hard-on."

Doris said nothing. She looked at the fire.

George looked at her look at the fire.

"I wish you hadn't said that," she finally said.

"I'm—I'm sorry, Doris. I just—I just feel we should be totally honest with each other."

"Oh!" she said quickly. "No, it's not that. It's just . . . that I have to go to confession." She stood abruptly, and reached for her hat.

He stared at her, suddenly starting to laugh. The laugh had to pass through so many giant lumps in his throat, it came out bumpy. He heard it, and tried to push it out harder, but the sound only tumbled out *hard* and bumpy. "This is really terribly funny, you know."

"Tell me—I could really use a good laugh."

"We're both crazy! We're really crazy! This kind of thing happens every day! To millions of people! I mean, we're just perfectly normal, healthy people who just did a perfectly normal, healthy thing! . . . You don't use actual names in confession, do you?"

"Of course not. Don't be silly."

"Thank God." He buried his face in his hands and massaged his eyebrows. He looked through his fingers. "You wanna hear my theory on sex and marriage?"

"I don't want to miss confession, George."

"Listen. Just listen. I mean, after you listen, you might not even need to *go* to confession."

Doris sat doubtfully down at the dresser.

He tucked his legs into lotus position, lit a cigarette, and blew out a ring. "Look. Suppose you compare a husband or a wife to a good book. So you got this great book and you read it—it's terrific. You love it. So you read the book again. *Still* good. So you read it again and again and again and even after maybe a hundred times, you still enjoy it. Well, you know the book by heart now, so for a little variety, you read it standing up, then lying down, then upside down, backwards, sideways, every way you can think of. You still like it, but Jesus, how many ways are there to read a book? Just once in a while you want to hear a new story, right? It doesn't mean you *hate* the old book. You'll read it again—later in the week. Who knows? Maybe you'll appreciate it more." He looked at her earnestly. "You understand what I'm saying, Doris?"

"No use crying over spilt milk?"

"Dammit, Doris!" He jumped to his feet. "You missed the whole point!"

"What was the point?"

"The point is—the *point* is—" He wheeled on her, stopped, "I've got to go to bed with you, right now!" He pulled her by the arm, and up to a kiss. He felt he was going to die from that kiss.

"George," she was pulling away, "we can't!"

"My God. Why not?"

"My God. You'll feel even worse afterwards."

"No. I won't." He kissed her again. "I won't, I won't. I'm over that now. I just"—he kissed her—"I just"—he kissed her—"remembered something."

"What?"

He kissed her.

"What?"

"Listen—"

"What?"

"I remembered—the Russians have the bomb! We could all be dead tomorrow!"

"George. Oh, George—you're clutching at straws!"

"Don't you understand?" He looked her in the eyes. "We're both mature, grown-up people with absolutely nothing to be afraid of!"

He kissed her. His heart pounded louder than—a door? Oh, Christ. There was somebody pounding on the door. He froze; the door pounded louder than a heart.

"What's that?" Doris whispered.

"I don't know." He suddenly dove to the floor, picked up her shoes. "Just a second!" he yelled, as she picked up her hat and ran for the bathroom. "No!" he yelled and then covered his mouth. "Don't go to the bathroom," he whispered.

"Why not?"

"It's the first place they look—Just a *second*!" he yelled at the menacing door, behind which waited J. Edgar Hoover, Jiminy Cricket, and Howard Duff. "*I'm coming!*" he pointed at the open window, and Doris followed his finger and ran. She was out on the patio. George looked around. Her girdle! He mangled it into his pocket. "I'm coming!" he hollered, and opened the door.

Old Man Chalmers stood in the doorway. Chalmers stood there holding a tray.

"What—what is it?" George whispered, and Chalmers squinted.

"Well," Chalmers said. "I think it's Wheaties. Then again, it might be Corn Flakes or Pep. All that little brown stuff looks alike. The yellow stuff's eggs—that I'm pretty sure of, and the—"

"Oh," George brightened. "Breakfast."

"Yep."

"*Thanks,* Mr. Chalmers." George scooped the tray

up and practically tripped in his hurry to turn. Chalmers just stood there, holding the door.

"I suppose you feel pretty proud of yourself."

"*What?*" George turned again, turning to ash.

"Not everyone could guess it was breakfast right off."

"*What?*" George repeated.

"Just a joke, Mr. Peters. I guess you're like Maggie. Kinda fuddled in the morning. Enjoy your breakfast."

Chalmers walked off.

George slammed the door, and then leaned up against it, exhaling a giant breath of relief. He crossed to the window and peered out. "Doris?"

Nothing.

Behind him, a deep voice growled, "Hah! So you've got a woman in here!"

Jumping, he bumped his head on the sill.

Doris stood there, hatted and barefoot, giggling slightly.

"It's all right," he told her. "I was calm. He didn't suspect a thing."

She watched as he put the tray on the table, and nodded slowly. "You mean—he didn't even ask about your girdle?"

"Huh?"

She was pointing down at his pocket, out of which sprouted garters and lace. "Oh great! Now he probably thinks I'm a homo. Jesus!" He tossed the thing on the bed.

"So?" She seemed to be wildly amused, which did not amuse him. She sat on the couch. "So what do you care?"

"I *care* because I have to see him every year."

"Every year?"

"Every year until the government stops collecting taxes. See, I have this friend who went into the wine business here. So I fly out this same weekend every year to do his books."

"From New Jersey?"

"Yeah. Well—see, we were in the army together, and

he was my first client. It's kind of—kind of a sentimental thing."

"Oh."

She was looking adorable again. Sitting on the couch with a silly straw hat, she seemed so . . . innocent. "Doris," he said, "Doris, there's something I want to tell you."

"What?"

"Well, I know you think I do this sort of thing all the time. I mean, I know I must appear very smooth and glib—sexually. Well, I want you to know that since I've been married, this is the very first time I've done this." He looked at her earnestly. "I hope you believe me."

"Sure. I could tell. Hey, listen, you mind if I share your breakfast?"

"Go on. Help yourself. You know, it's really funny. Even when I was single I was no good at quick, superficial affairs. I had to be able to really *like* the person before—what the hell do you mean, you could tell?"

"Hmm? Oh. I dunno. The way you tried to get your pants off over your shoes and then tripped and hit your head on the coffee table?" She smiled at him fondly. "Little things like that."

"Oh." Shrugging, he smiled at her. "Well . . . listen, I'm glad I told you, anyway. I mean, it feels great to be totally honest with another person. Doesn't it?"

"Mmm." She smiled through toast.

"I haven't been totally honest, Doris."

"You haven't?"

"No." He took a deep breath. "I said I was a married man with two children."

"You're not?"

"I'm a married man with *three* children."

She frowned. "I don't get it."

"I thought it would make me seem less married."

She stopped eating and stared at him now. "Look," he flushed, "I just didn't think it all the way through! Anyway, it's been like a lead weight inside me all morning. I mean, denying little Debbie like that. I'm sorry,

Doris. I was under a certain stress or I wouldn't have done it. You understand?"

She nodded. "We all do dopey things. Sometimes." She smiled. "You want some Wheaties?"

"No." He paced to the fireplace and back. By the time he'd got back she'd finished the Wheaties and started the eggs. "How come your wife doesn't travel with you?"

"Huh? Oh. Phyllis won't get on a plane."

"She's afraid of flying?"

"Crashing."

"Oh. . . . Why are you *looking* at me like that?"

"Nothing. I just love the way you eat."

"Oh." She put down the fork. "Too much. I eat too much?"

"No! It's not a question of quantity, Doris. It's a question of . . . quality. You have a certain quality when you eat. A certain . . . exuberance. I love that."

"You're crazy."

"I know. And I'm normally terribly sane. Doris, you just *do* things to me." He sat down beside her. "Doris—do you believe that two total strangers can look at each other across a crowded room and suddenly want to possess each other in every conceivable, possible way?"

She hesitated, with toast in the air, thinking it over. "Uh-uh," she said, and ate the toast.

"Then how the hell did this whole thing start?"

"When you sent me that steak." She looked at him now. "What made you do it?"

He shrugged. "I don't know. Impulse. Usually I never do that kind of thing. I have this—this friend who says life is saying 'yes.' I don't know," he shrugged again. "The most I can generally manage is a 'maybe.' "

"So why'd you do it?"

"I guess I was lonely and you looked so—so vulnerable, and—well, you had a run in your stocking and your lipstick was smeared and—"

"You thought I looked cheap?"

"No! Beautiful! I'm *attracted* by flaws. I don't know—somehow they make people seem more human and—approachable. That's why I like Pete Reiser better than say, Joe DiMaggio. I mean, Reiser keeps running into walls. I like that."

"You know something, George? You're a real nice guy." They smiled at each other. He moved to kiss her. "What made you think I was a medium rare?"

"I'm very intuitive."

"I'm well-done."

"What?" He pulled back. "You're well-*done*? How could anybody like their meat well-done?"

"Harry always has his that way."

"Oh." He absently reached for some toast. "What were you doing in the restaurant anyway?"

"Oh. I was lost."

"On your way to where?"

"Well . . ." she flushed, "it didn't seem right to bring it up last night but—well, I was on my way to a retreat."

He choked. "You're kidding."

"No. Catholic."

"You're serious."

"Sure. It's right nearby. On Route twenty-nine. I go every year on this same weekend. See, this is Harry's mother's birthday and he always takes the kids to Bakersfield to see her. So I came here."

"And she doesn't mind that you don't go there?"

"Oh no," Doris laughed. "She absolutely hates me because I got pregnant."

"Her son had something to do with that, too."

"I think she sort of blocks that out of her mind. Listen, I don't blame her. You see, Harry was in his first year of dental college, and he had to drop out and sell waterless cooking. Anyway, the point is, every year on her birthday, I go on a retreat."

He thought about that. "You mean you just sit and think about God?"

"Yeah. Well. Him, too. But more about—well, myself." She sat on the sofa again. "You see . . . see, I got pregnant when I was just eighteen, so I never really had any time to—well—to think about . . . what I think. Oh, I don't know what I'm trying to say. Sometimes I think I'm crazy."

"Why?"

"Well, I mean . . . take a look at my life. I live in a two-bedroom duplex in downtown Oakland. We have a nineteen-forty-eight Kaiser that's almost paid for, a blond three-piece dinette set, a Motorola TV, and we go out bowling at least once a week. I mean, what else could anyone ask for?" She frowned. "But sometimes things get me down, you know? It's dumb!"

"No. I don't think it's dumb, Doris."

"You don't?"

He shook his head at her.

"Boy . . . you know sometimes I think I'm even too dumb to know what's dumb. I mean, here I am—" She stopped. "Oh boy. Will you listen to me? Gee . . . I can really talk to you, George. I mean, I find myself saying things to you . . . I mean, things that I didn't even think that I thought. I noticed that right away when we met."

"Yeah. I know. We had instant rapport. Did you notice that too?"

"No. But I know we really hit it off." She smiled. "Harry isn't much of a talker. . . . What about your wife? Do you two . . . talk a lot?"

George frowned. It suddenly seemed that reporting on Helen was worse betrayal than cheating on her. "Doris, look—" He got up to pace. "Naturally, we're both curious about each other's husband and wife. But rather than, well, *dwelling* on it, and letting it spoil everything, why don't we do this? I'll tell you two stories—one showing the best side of my wife and the other showing the worst. Then you do the same about your husband, and then let's *forget* that. Okay?"

"Okay."

"Okay. I'll go first. I'll start with the worst side of her first." He sighed. "Phyllis *knows* about us."

"Come on, George. You said that before. Now how could she know?"

"Well . . . she's got this—thing in her head."

"You mean like a plate?"

He turned. "Plate?"

"Yeah. My uncle has one of those. He was wounded in the war and they put this steel plate in his head, and now he says he can always tell when it's going to rain." She was serious.

"Oh. Oh boy." He stared. "Oh boy, I am really in a *lot* of trouble."

"Why?"

"Because I find everything you say absolutely *fascinating*."

"Oh." She smiled. "So tell me about your wife's steel plate."

"What? Oh. It isn't a plate. It's more like . . . a bell. I mean, I could be a million miles away, but whenever I even *look* at another woman, that bell goes off like a fire alarm. Last night at one twenty-two, I just know she sat bolt upright in bed with her head going ding-ding-ding-ding-ding-ding-ding!"

"How did you know it was one twenty-two?"

"I have peripheral vision, and I noticed my watch said four fifty-seven."

"That's crazy."

"Okay. I happen to have personal idiosyncracies and I happen to like my watch to be—"

"No, I didn't mean that. I mean about your wife's fire bell and all."

"Look," he said testily, "I certainly realize the bell isn't real, but on the other hand it's terribly real to *me*."

"I'm sorry. Listen . . . now tell me something nice about her."

"Huh? Oh—well . . ." he softened, "well . . . she made me believe in myself. You see," he paced, and chewed at his nail, "it's probably hard for you to imagine, but I used to be horribly insecure."

"And how did she make you believe in yourself?"

"She married me."

"Oh. That was nice of her. . . . I mean, bolstering you up, and all."

"Yeah." He grinned, and sat on the couch. "Okay. Your turn. Worst first."

"Huh?"

"Tell me the worst story first."

"Oh . . ." She was thinking. "Well . . ." She was thinking. "Gee . . ." She was thinking. "Gee, that's hard."

"To pick one?"

"To think of one. Harry's really the salt of the earth—everyone says so."

"Listen," he snapped. "You owe me at least one rotten story."

"Well . . . okay. This isn't really rotten but, well—on our fourth anniversary we were having kind of a rough time. The kids were getting us down and—well, we'd gotten over our heads financially but we decided to have some friends over anyway, and the thing is, well, Harry doesn't drink very much, but that night he had a couple of beers—after the Gilette fights?—and anyway, he started talking to the guys—and—well—what I overheard him say"—she paused—"he said his time in the army was the best time of his life."

"So?" George frowned at her. "What's wrong with that? I mean, a lot of guys feel that way about the service."

"Yeah. But Harry was in the army for four years. And three of them were spent in a Japanese prison camp! And he said this on our anniversary! Oh, I know he didn't mean to hurt me—Harry would never hurt anyone—but well, it . . . hurt, you know?" She looked in his eyes. "You're the only person I've ever told." She held his eyes for a long moment. "Now you want to hear the good one about him?"

"No."

"You have to. I mean, I don't want you to get the wrong impression."

"Okay. If you insist."

"Well—Harry's this really big, kind of heavyset guy, you know?"

"I wish you hadn't told me that."

"Oh, don't worry. He's gentle as—as a puppy. Anyway, he tries to be with all the kids—separately, you know, and do different things with them. So, anyway, he was having this hard time finding something special to do with Tony, our four-year old. So then, last winter, he gets this idea to take him to the park and fly this big kite. Well, he tells Tony about it—really builds it up—and Tony gets real excited. So this one Saturday last winter they go out together, but there's no wind, and Harry has trouble getting the kite to even take off. Well, it's kind of cold and Tony, who's pretty bored by now—he's only four years old—asks if he can sit in the car, and Harry says, 'Sure.' " She started to smile. "So about an hour later, I happen to come by on my way from the laundromat and I see Tony, asleep in the car, and Harry, all red in the face, and all out of breath, pounding up and down, all alone in the park, with this giant kite just dragging behind him." Her smile faded. She shrugged. "Well, I don't know—it just really got to me . . . you know?"

He looked at her; he didn't find the story terribly touching, but he found her reaction to the story touching.

"Yeah," he said defensively, "well, *Helen* has some pretty nice qualities too."

She frowned. "Who's Helen?"

"My wife, of course."

"You said her name was Phyllis."

He closed his eyes, and nodded. "I lied." He rallied. "Phyllis—Helen—hell, what's the difference? I'm *married*! Look, I'm sorry. I was nervous, and I just didn't want to leave any *clues*. I mean I was scared you'd try to look me up—or something."

She watched him with slow dismay. "Is your name really George?"

"Of course! You think I'd lie about my *name*?"

She nodded. "You're crazy." She shrugged. "I guess maybe we're both crazy."

They smiled at each other. "Funny," he said. "Here we are, in a strange hotel room, gazing into each other's eyes, and we're both married with six kids between us."

She grinned. "You got pictures?"

"What?"

"Of your kids."

"Oh. Well, *sure*. But Jesus, Doris. I hardly think this is the time or the place to—"

"I'll show you mine if you show me yours." She reached for her bag. "I keep them in this special folder we got free from Kodak." She pulled out the black plastic folder. "Here. Where are yours?"

"Oh." He fumbled in his pocket. "Well, you have to take the whole wallet." He handed it to her, cursing himself for the momentary fear that she'd note his address, call up Helen, threaten blackmail, or charge something up on his Bamberger's card. He hurriedly put it out of his mind and looked at her look at his family album.

"Oh, they're really *cute*," she crooned. "Is this one here with the glasses the oldest?"

"Yeah. That's Michael. Funny-looking, isn't he?"

"He wants to be Superman?"

"Sometimes it worries me. . . . Hey—" he was looking at the Kodak folder. The ugliest kid he'd ever seen in his life. "Why is this one's face screwed up?"

"Huh?" She peered at the picture. "Oh. That's Tony—it was taken on a roller coaster. Isn't it natural-looking?" She smiled. "Exactly right after that, he threw up."

"He's really . . . something," George said nicely. "I guess he looks kind of like Harry, huh?"

"Like both of us, really. . . . What's your little girl's name?"

"Debbie." He laughed. "That one was taken on her second birthday. We were trying to get her to blow out the candles."

"She's got her hand in the middle of the cake."

"Yeah. *Neat* is not her strong suit."

They smiled at each other.

George started smelling hibiscus again.

"You have great-looking kids, George."

"Yeah. You too."

"Thanks."

He could feel the sand underneath him start shifting again. He reached over slowly, cupping her chin. He kissed her. She kissed him, tenderly, back. They pulled apart; they smiled at each other.

"All *right*," she said mournfully, holding the smile and undoing her blouse, "all right. But this is the last time. . . ."

compliments of:
OAKLAND FIDELITY TRUST

"Time is $"

Week of Feb. 19, 1956

Sun.

Mon.

Tues.

Wed.

Thurs.

Fri. Harry's Mother's Birthday

Sat.

FIVE

At one o'clock on Friday afternoon, Doris entered the chic, sleek, bustling lobby of San Francisco's Fairmont Hotel. A very slim, blond woman in a taupe suit was walking towards her. Doris smiled. The woman smiled. Doris admired the woman's looks, and then was surprised, as she often was, to learn this admirable creature was Doris. Face to face with herself in the mirror, she ran a hand through her ash-blond hair, smiled again at her reedlike shape, and quickly crossed to the restaurant door.

Liz was there at a corner table, under the shade of a picture hat. "I already ordered martinis," she said, as Doris sat in the wine-colored booth. " 'Dry,' I said to the waiter. 'Dry. I want them so dry there's dust on the olives.' "

"Mmmm." Doris sipped, and then screwed up her face. She put down the glass. "I hate martinis. You think they'd throw me out if I ordered a beer?"

"Probably."

"Oh."

"Don't worry. I'll drink it. This is a two-martini day." Liz looked baleful.

"Roger didn't call," Doris concluded.

Nodding slowly, Liz ate her olive. "I think I'll become a belated nun."

"As long as they'd let you out once a week to get your hair done. Come on, Liz."

"I'm serious, Doris. In five years I've had three lovers, and what have I got to show for it all?—A couple of luggage stickers from Havana, and a swizzle stick from The Top of the Mark. *I* don't know . . ." Liz sipped her drink, "sometimes I think I should have married Bill."

"Well," Doris said, "you didn't love him."

"I know," Liz sighed, "but gee, I don't know . . . there's a lot be be said for not being in love. I'd really like to get my hands on the neck of the person who told me love was such *fun*."

"I know," Doris said.

"How could you know? I mean Harry's a sweet, wonderful guy. Me, I got a talent for picking louses. Louses and rats. And the thing is, I really thought Roger was different. I mean, my God," she reached for some nuts, "who'd ever guess you could meet a rat at a *Stevenson* rally?"

Doris nodded.

Liz shook her head and lit up a Kent, from the wrong end. She smoked it for a while before she noticed, and stubbed it out.

"He's making you that unhappy, huh?"

"You want to know *how* uphappy, Doris?" Liz was pointing at the side of her eye. "I'm getting a line."

"Where?"

"Here." She poked a nail at her face.

Doris squinted. "I can't see it."

"Well of course you can't *see* it." Liz looked appalled. "My God, if you could *see* it, I'd *hang* myself, Doris. But the point is, it's there. I'm thirty years old. Oh, Doris, you don't know how lucky you are. You're married. You don't have to think about love." She grabbed the second martini and drank.

Doris stared at a corner table. A dark-haired girl in a yellow dress was gazing raptly at the eyes of a man. They were holding hands.

Doris grabbed her martini back. "Liz," she said, "I've got something to tell you." Doris drank. The whole glass.

Liz leaned forward. "Jesus. It must be a helluva story." Frowning, she reached for Doris's hand. "What's the matter, Doris?"

"I—" Doris paused. She desperately needed someone to talk to, but talking about it seemed so—wrong. And besides, what would happen if she just came out with it, just said, "Liz—I'm having an affair"? Would Liz purse her lips, narrow her eyes, beetle her eyebrows, straighten her spine and say, "Doris, you horrid contemptible woman, Doris, you sinner, you must give him up"? Would Liz say something constructive like that? Not on your life. She'd probably say, "That's wonderful, Doris. Tell me about it. When did you meet?"

"Five years ago," Doris would *wail*. "And I've been meeting him once a year ever since. The weekend I'm supposed to go on retreat. Only, I don't go on retreat. I go on a wild, crazy weekend. We drink champagne and have breakfast in bed and he takes me dancing and sometimes I'm even afraid that I love him and that's so awful I'm breaking it off."

"You're what?"

"I'm not showing up this year. I'm honestly going to *go* on retreat, and I'm never going to see him again."

Liz would undoubtedly cock her head. "Doris," she'd say, "I think you're crazy. I mean, if Harry doesn't find out and you're having a wonderful time with this guy, who's it hurting?"

Doris had already spent seven months asking and trying to answer that question. The closest thing to an answer she'd gotten was, "Gee, I don't know. But that's like saying, if no one finds out, it's perfectly ducky to rob a bank," to which Liz would then answer, "You mean it isn't?"

No. Talking to Liz wouldn't help. But Liz was now sitting here waiting to listen, leaning forward and looking concerned. "Doris," she said now, slightly perplexed at Doris's long, dreamy silence, "you said you wanted to tell me something?"

"I—" Doris started, "I—" she continued, "I—" she hesitated, "I—" she tried, "I—" she decided, "just bought a wonderful dress on sale. Black. Silk. It's a Suzy Perrette with a low-cut—"

"Doris?"

If you're going to break it off, Liz would say, *the least you should do is show up, Doris—in a black, silk, low-cut dress."*

"Oh no," Doris said, out loud. "I can't."

"You can't?" Liz repeated, completely confused.

I can't, Doris thought. If I saw him we'd just have a horrible scene and I'd hurt him and I don't want to hurt him, Liz.

"You can't *what*?" Liz demanded. "Doris? Are you sure you're feeling okay?"

On the other hand, Doris suddenly thought with the instant clarity often provided by a strong martini on an empty stomach—on the other hand, she owed it to George to show up. If she didn't show up, that would hurt him more. She knew because she pictured it the other way around. If *she* were up there, sitting in the cottage, waiting, watching the clock hands move, pacing, moaning, biting her nails, afraid to leave, afraid to stay—no, she couldn't do that to George. She'd face him, squarely, like an adult—in a low-cut, black, Suzy Perrette, with satin slippers and loads of perfume.

"Excuse me," she said, and got to her feet, the martini practically knocking her down, "if I'm going, I have to go home and bake."

"And bake?" Liz was looking terribly concerned.

"It's the weekend I go on retreat," Doris said, "and I forgot to bake Harry's mother a cake. You see," she hiccoughed and nervously laughed, "if I'd known I were going, I'd have baked a cake."

"Doris?" Liz said. "Are you *sure* you're okay . . . ?"

SIX

"And a cake, Mr. Chalmers." George Peters leaned on the counter. "Could you send me over a chocolate cake? With five candles."

"Five candles," Angus repeated.

Peters flushed. "It's my daughter's birthday," he added quickly, "and I thought I'd just celebrate, quietly, alone in my room."

Angus nodded, chewing his lip. "Mr. Peters—George—would it make it—would it make it any easier for you if I told you that, well—when I was your age, *I* had a five-year-old daughter too?"

"Huh?"

"She was twenty and her name was Marie. She sang with the Bozo Mulligan Band. They played in Frisco."

"Oh."

"I just thought you might like to know."

Peters gave it thought for a moment. "Mr. Chalmers . . ." He leaned over closer the desk. "Mr. Chalmers, could—could I ask you a question?"

"You mean, did my wife ever find out?"

Peters nodded.

Angus shook his head. "Nope. Not then or the next time either."

"There were others?"

"One. I guess it was August of forty-two. I was pretty upset because they wouldn't draft me. She was twenty years old and her name was Arlette. A riveter from Long Beach." Angus smiled. "I had terrible taste in Other Women." He laughed. "Well, I just thought you might like to know. I mean—so you can order *two* cups of coffee with you four eggs, eight slices of bacon and seven pieces of toast in the morning."

"Thanks, Mr. Chalmers." Peters smiled and straightened his tie. "It's really a giant load off my mind to know—to know that we're both . . . Men Of The World."

"Of The World," Angus said, and nodded slowly. "Now let me just get this order straight. You want orange crepe paper, seven balloons, and a chocolate cake with five candles . . . ?"

Angus watched as Peters left. He was looking a little more prosperous now: gray-flannel suit, pink Oxford shirt, wine-colored tie. Angus remembered himself at that age: double-breasted pinstripe, navy blue shirt, cream-colored tie. And Marie—all skinny and Harlow-blonde. And Maggie—his one-of-a-kind Maggie—six months pregnant with Annabelle then. Two pregnancies right in a row, and Angus had briefly required Marie . . . Lafollette? . . . La Marca? . . . DeLuca? . . . DeLowe . . . ? Damned if he even remembered her name. . . .

"Dollar for your thoughts," Maggie was saying.

"Huh? Oh." Angus looked up. For a moment, Maggie looked Harlow-blonde, and it took him a second to register, again, that the platinum color of her hair was *white*. "I was thinking of sending Larry to town to buy some balloons."

"Balloons?" She tilted her platinum head.

"For George Peters. . . . Larry around?"

"Mmm. Passed a window and saw him out back."

"With Joanna?"

"Uh-huh." Maggie smiled. "I think we could call him 'otherwise engaged.' "

Angus grinned. "Christ, I hope so. Maybe he's finally come to his senses. Stop acting like he's the only man in the world ever to lose an arm in a war."

"Mmm. Well, Joanna's just what he needed, and while you're in town to shop for balloons, will you get me a copy of *Bridey Murphy*?"

"No," Angus muttered, grabbing his coat. "I will not be *seen* with that idiot book. Reincarnation! Jesus Christ. . . . All right," he muttered, taking the keys, "but I'll come back to haunt you."

Margaret laughed.

She took his position behind the desk and watched as he made his way to the lot. Pulling in was a Nash coupé. A blond with a small overnight bag got out of the car and walked to the porch.

"Hi," she said, when she got to the desk.

Margaret smiled. "Hello, Mrs. Smith. Good to see you again."

"Yes." Mrs. Smith was chewing her lip. "You have my single room with a bath?"

"Of course." Margaret hesitated a second. "Mrs. Smith," she decided, "there's something—there's something I'd like to tell you."

"Oh?" Mrs. Smith looked up nervously.

"Well," Margaret said, "would it make it—would it make it any easier for you, if I told you that—well—that *my* name used to be Mrs. Smith too?"

"Hmm?"

"Of course I was older than you. Angus was having a bing with a riveter, and I was—I guess I was forty years old. The point is—you're wasting money on a room and you could use the money and we could use the room."

"Oh." Mrs. Smith stopped biting her lip. "Oh." She flushed; then she frowned. "Mrs. Chalmers, could I ask—could I ask you something?"

"Of course, Mrs. Smith."

"Doris."

"Doris."

"Did you still love your husband—and the other man too?"

"I never stopped loving Angus for a minute. And he's never stopped—well—thrilling me, either. But Angus was so . . . articulate, you know? And at that time, I needed somebody quiet. Someone who didn't understand me at all. Someone who'd find me . . .

mysterious. . . . Well . . ." Margaret tried to focus on Henry McGuire. "I suppose I loved him for *being* there at the right time, but I can't say I really *loved* him . . ." She shrugged. "Well, anyway, I thought it might help you to know."

"Oh. Well . . . thank you, Mrs. Chalmers."

"Margaret."

"Margaret." Doris smiled, and picked up her bag. Mrs. Chalmers had really meant well, but Doris wasn't really sure what it *meant,* or more precisely, what it meant to Doris. It dawned on her slowly as she crossed the lobby that you couldn't find your morals in other people's stories. You had to find your own; and then you had to build your own story around them. It wasn't a question of what Liz would do, or Grace Kelly, or Madame Bovary, or Marjorie Morningstar, or Mrs. Chalmers. Doris had to do what *Doris* had to do. And that was that. She walked through the lobby and out to the porch and out through the garden and out past a bench where Larry Chalmers was kissing a girl in a tree-shaded nook, in a twilight lit by a single star.

Approaching the cottage, she wondered what the hell it was she had to do.

SEVEN

Doris slowly stepped from the tub, reached for a towel, and started running a brush through her hair. She wasn't sure if he liked her hair. He'd said he liked it, but that didn't count. He'd walked through the door with a bunch of flowers he'd picked from the garden, looked at her, dropped the flowers and his jaw, and muttered, "My God. It's Doris Day."

"Gina Lollobrigida," Doris had said.

"She's a brunette."

"Quibbler!" Doris accused. They'd kissed. She'd felt herself melting to chocolate sauce. George had then suddenly pulled from her arms, and blathered a "Why don't you go take a bath?"

"A *bath*?"

"Or a walk."

"A *bath*?"

"Would you just leave the room for a while?"

"Do I smell?"

"Oh, Doris. You smell terrific. You look terrific. I love your hair. Would you just leave the *room*?"

She'd frowned.

He'd kissed her. "Listen," he whispered, "I've got a surprise. Will you just disappear so you'll be surprised?"

"Oh."

She'd gone in to take a bath.

She'd heard Mr. Chalmers come, and go. She now heard the radio saying, ". . . *and—fair—, at eight o'clock.*" The dial was turned. A newscaster said, ". . . *at the Fresno Stevenson rally tonight* . . ." Doris reached for her bracelet. She took in a deep, painful breath and held it, as the Fresno rallyers sang (to the tune of "My Darling Clementine"):

I'm an egghead, I'm an egghead,
I'm an egghead, happ-i-ly.
But I'd rather be an egghead,
Than a bone-head G.O.P.
I'm an egg—

The dial was suddenly turned. Holding her breath, she hooked up the bra. Nelson Riddle played "Love And Marriage." The dial was suddenly turned—off.

"Damn!"

"What's the matter?" George called in.

"It's my Merry Widow."

"Your what?" he hollered.

"My Merry Widow." Doris was pulling her dress from the hook. "It's a cross between a bra and the Spanish Inquisition. It mashes you in and pushes you out. It also gives you this pale, wan look, because it's cutting off all of your circulation."

"Oh. Let me know when you're coming in."

She finished zipping the back of her black, low-cut dress, and clipped on a pair of rhinestone earrings. "Okay. Now."

"No! Not yet."

She waited.

"Okay," he hollered. "Now."

She entered the room as George, sitting at the small piano, played a few chords and started to sing: "If I Knew You Were Coming, I'd Have Baked A Cake." Laughing, she looked around at the room. Seven balloons were tied to the bed. Orange crepe paper streamed from the mantle. A champagne bucket rested on the hearth, and a cake on the table in front of the couch. A sign said *Happy Anniversary, Darling*. It was gorgeously stupid. She loved it.

"Oh, George."

He finished singing and kissed her again. And again. "Happy anniversary, darling." Grinning, he pointed down at the cake. "Cut it," he said, "and make a wish."

She moved to the couch, picked up the knife and stared at the candles for several seconds. Closing her eyes, she blew them all out.

"What did you wish?" He sat beside her with a glass of champagne.

She sipped it thoughtfully, then put it down, and started cutting a wedge from the cake. "I have only one wish."

"What?"

"That you keep showing up every year."

He grinned, and kissed her.

She served him some cake.

He put down the plate. "That was one of the best ideas you ever had."

"What? Meeting you here every year?"

"Refusing to run away with me, Doris. I asked you to. Remember?"

"Oh sure. Tahiti. And then you decided you'd want to bring Michael and you worried about the *schools* in Tahiti. Oh, George. You've matured a lot since then."

He smiled. "So have you."

"Oh dear."

"I mean, in a good way, Doris." He frowned. "Weren't you even tempted?"

"To run away with you? Sure, I was. I still am. But I had the feeling if we'd run off together, we'd have ended up—well, with pretty much the same sort of comfortable marriage that both of us already had at home."

"Maybe." He drank. "But I have a confession. I feel kind of nice and comfortable *here.* Boy, the first year I was really a wreck. I mean, I was certain you wouldn't show up."

"I know. I didn't think you'd come either."

"In fact, I worried the second year too. And the third. And a little bit on the fourth." He paused. "Of course in those days, I had less confidence in my personal magnetism."

"Mmm. But this year, you knew I was coming."

"Oh, yeah. Didn't have a doubt in the world."

She nodded, cutting herself some cake. "Where did you get the cake?" she said brightly.

"Chalmers brought it. While you were changing."

"Mmm. Isn't that a bit . . . risky?"

"Well," he was pouring some more champagne, "I wouldn't be surprised if old man Chalmers had figured things out."

"Yeah. I wouldn't be surprised if he had." She licked some chocolate icing from her nail, and looked up to find him staring again. She nodded. "You really hate my hair."

"I already told you—I *love* your hair."

"Mmm. I don't know . . ." she moved to the mirror, and looked at herself. "Maybe next time, I should go to the city to have it done . . ."

"How *are* the suburbs?"

She turned. "Muddy. Right now everyone's very excited because *next* week they're going to connect the sewers." She shrugged, and crossed to the sofa again. "It's not exactly the life of Scott and Zelda, but we're surviving."

"You started reading!" He beamed at her.

"Yeah. Oh listen, you don't know the half of it, George. I joined the Book-of-the-Month Club."

"Great! Good for you."

"And not only that," she said wryly, "sometimes I even take the *alternate* selections."

"I'm really proud of you, honey."

She grinned. "Well . . . it was that, or mambo lessons. Listen, before we demolish that cake, you want to have dinner?"

"You mean, in the dining room? Just like grown-ups?"

"Well, as long as our secret is out."

"Sure. I mean, seeing you're all dressed up, I guess I'm selfish to keep you to myself."

Crossing the garden, George held her hand, and Doris felt guilt twinging her happiness; she briefly remembered her firm resolution to break things off. She broke off a twig from a eucalyptus, just as they started to enter the lobby.

Old Man Chalmers sat at the desk. He smiled at her nicely, and Doris was aware that she hadn't flushed. She wondered if that was a sign of maturity. Or debauchery. She looked up at George, who squeeed her hand.

"Hey, where's Albert?" George was saying to the very young waiter.

"Dead," said the very young man, abstractly. "Would you like a cocktail?"

"No. Champagne and a couple of menus."

"Any particular kind you'd like?"

"Red plastic, I think would be fine. If you meant the champagne, how about a Bella Blanc des Blancs?"

The waiter nodded and walked away.

Doris said, "We ought to drink to him, shouldn't we?"

"Albert, yeah."

"Well, him too. I was really thinking of your friend Bella. For bringing us together."

"Speaking of which, I got here Wednesday and finished his books. We can have the whole thirty-six hours together."

The waiter came back and served the champagne. "To Bella." Doris lifted her glass.

"To absent waiters." George lifted his.

They drank.

Doris said, "Is it warm in here?"

"No. I don't think so." He opened his menu.

"Oh . . ." she said. "Is it cold in New Jersey? I mean was it snowing or something when you—"

"Oh." He looked up. "I forgot to tell you. We moved to Connecticut."

"Really?"

"Yeah. We bought an old barn and converted it."

"Oh." She opened her menu. "What's it like?"

"Drafty. And Helen's got the decorating bug." George looked up from his menu again. "I'm getting this mental image of Helen, standing at my funeral, just as they're closing the lid on my coffin, throwing in two swatches of fabric, and yelling, *'Which one do you like?'* " He grinned. "That's my bad story about her."

Doris laughed. "So what else is new?"

"A baby. We had a new baby. A girl."

"Oh George." She was beaming. "Congratulations. You have a picture?"

"I knew you'd ask." He brought out some snapshots and handed them to her. A sweet, plump, pink baby gurgled at her from out of a crib. "Oh, she's adorable," Doris grinned, and slowly handed the pictures back. "It's funny . . . I still like to look at babies, but I don't want to *own* one anymore. You think that's a sign of maturity?"

"Maybe." George was producing a large cigar. "Listen, I even kept one of these, for you to give Harry . . . It's from Havana."

"Harry still thinks I go on retreat. What should I tell him?—I got the cigar from a Cuban nun?"

"Oh." He laughed, and let the cigar drop to the table. "Is it warm in here?"

"No. I don't think so. Listen, how are the rest of the kids? How's Michael?"

"Crazy as ever. He had this homework assignment to write what he did on his summer vacation. Trouble is, he chose to write what he actually did."

"And what was that?"

"Tried to get laid. He wrote in great, comic detail about his unfortunate tendency to get an erection on all forms of public transportation. They almost expelled him." George was laughing.

"You're really crazy about him, aren't you."

"Well . . . he's a very weird kid, Doris."

"And he really gets to you. Come on—admit it."

He looked at her. "Yeah. Okay. I admit it. He's a nice kid."

"See?" she said gently. "Was that so hard?"

He leaned across the table and suddenly kissed her. "Hey, what was *that* for?"

"Everything. This. One beautiful weekend every

year, with no cares, no ties, no responsibilities. . . . Thank you, darling." They looked at each other.

The waiter said, "Have you decided what you want?"

They both nodded, and very slowly got up from the table.

"Gee," Doris laughed, as they raced through the garden, "gee, and I just got all dressed up."

They were half-undressed, when the telephone rang. They were lying on the bed. It rang again. George ignored it. Still, it rang. "Damn. Let it ring," George muttered hoarsely. "Probably only Tony Bella wanting to know what he owes the Feds."

The telephone rang.

Doris sighed. "Chalmers probably told him you're in."

"Dammit." George picked the phone up. "Hello?" He bolted upright in bed. "Yes, this is Daddy. Is anything wrong?—*Funny?*" She watched him with steady eyes. He was red and pale at the same time. "Well, that's probably because Daddy was just—uh—I had a frog in my throat, sweetheart." He bent over double, clutching the phone, almost as though he had pains in his stomach. Sighing, Doris moved from the bed, starting to straighten her clothes and hair. "It came out, huh?" he said to the phone. "Well of *course* the tooth fairy will come. . . . Tonight. . . . Sure . . . It doesn't matter if you can't find it, darling. The tooth fairy will know . . . Well, I wish I could be there to find it for you, honey, but daddy's working. . . ." Doris moved to the sofa and sat. She toyed with a piece of the chocolate cake. "Yes . . . daddy's working in his room. . . . Yes, honey, it's a very nice room . . . Well, it has a fireplace and a sofa and a big comfortable b—bathroom. . . ." Doris walked into the bathroom. She ran some water over her wrists. "No, I'm afraid I can't come home, honey. You see, daddy has to finish his—business . . . well, I'll try. . . . Yes, sweetheart. I love you too. Yes, very much. . . ."

Doris heard the sound as he hung up the phone. She

counted to seven before she walked back to the bedroom again. He was sitting on the bed with his head in his hands.

"Oh, God. I feel so guilty!" he moaned.

"Debbie?"

He rose, and started to pace. "Her tooth came out. She can't find it and she's worried the tooth fairy won't know. Oh God, that thin, reedy little voice." He turned to Doris. "Do you know what that *does* to me?"

"Sure," Doris snapped. "That cheerful expression doesn't fool me for a minute."

"You think this is *funny*?" George wheeled around.

"Honey, honey," Doris said gently, "I know how you feel. Honest, I do. But I don't think it helps to go on and on and on about it."

"Doris," he wailed, "my little girl said 'I love you, Daddy,' and I answered in a voice still *hoarse with passion!*"

Doris sighed. "I think I've got the *pic*ture, George."

Her tone seemed to jolt him. He stared at her now. "God . . . don't *you* ever feel guilty?"

"Sometimes."

"You've never said anything."

"I just deal with it in a different way."

"How?"

"Privately."

"Hmmp. I don't know—" He started pacing. "Maybe men are more sensitive than women."

"Have a drink, George."

"I mean, women are more pragmatic than men."

"What's that supposed to mean?"

"It means they adjust to rottenness quicker." He shrugged. "Anyway, you've got the church."

"The *church*?"

He turned. "Well, you're Catholic, aren't you? You can get rid of all your guilt at one sitting. Me, I have to *live* with mine."

"Swell," she said tersely. "I think *I'll* have a drink." She walked to the piano and poured some champagne, drank it, and poured out another glass. When she'd finished that, he was still pacing.

"Boy," he was saying, "something like that really brings you up short." He held out a pair of trembling hands. "I mean *look* at me, Doris!" She looked, unimpressed. "I'm telling you, Doris," he shook his head, "when she started talking about the tooth fairy, well . . . " he sighed, "it affected me in a very profound manner." His hand had now wandered up to his heart. "And on top of that—I've got indigestion you wouldn't *believe*." He appealed to her. "It hit me that hard, you know?"

"George," she said flatly, "I've got three children too."

"Sure, sure, I know." He paced. "I don't mean to say that you don't *understand*. It's just that we're different people and your guilt is less—acute." He turned. He looked so poignantly dumb, pacing barefoot, with an open fly.

"Honey," she pleaded, "listen, what do you want to do? Have a guilt contest? Is that gonna help to *solve* anything?"

"What do you *want* me to do, Doris?"

"I think it might be a terrific idea if you just stopped talking about it, okay? It's only making you feel a lot worse."

"I *can't* feel worse."

She rolled her eyes.

"That pure little voice saying—"

"*Uch!*" She hadn't realized she'd *uch*ed out loud, but she'd *uch*ed out loud, and she wasn't sorry.

He stared at her. "No. You're right," he said. "You're right. Forget it. Come on. We'll talk about something else. Tell me your good Harry story."

She looked at him. Clearly, he was trying very hard. The least she could do was pull herself together and help him. "Okay," she let out a breath and put on a smile. "Harry went bankrupt."

"What?" That jolted him out of it. "Doris? How can anyone go bankrupt selling television sets?"

She shrugged. "Harry has this one, giant weakness as a salesman. It's a compulsion to talk people out of things they can't afford. He lacks the killer instinct." She smiled. "It's one of the things I like best about him. Anyway, he went into real estate. Now. Your turn."

"What?"

"Tell me your Helen story."

"I already did."

"You only told the bad one. Why do you always tell the bad one first?"

"It's the one I look forward to telling the most."

"Oh. Well, tell me the good story now."

"Well . . ." he was getting edgy again, Doris could tell, but still he was trying; again, he paced. "Well . . . Chris—that's our middle one—gashed his knee on a lawn sprinkler. Helen drove both of us to the hospital."

"Both of you?"

"I fainted." He shrugged. "And the nice part was that she never told anybody."

"Oh." Doris frowned. "You faint often?"

"Only in emergencies."

"Oh. Well, is it the sight of blood that—"

"*Please,* Doris. My stomach's squeamish enough already. Listen, maybe I will have that drink." He walked to the piano. Carefully avoiding the open champagne, he poured out some Scotch. "Listen," he said in a casual voice, "Um . . . something just occurred to me, Doris. Instead of my leaving at the usual time, would you mind if I left a little bit early?"

She was wary. "What did you have in mind?"

"Well, there's a plane in half an hour."

"You want to leave *thirty-five hours* early?" She stood with her arms crossed on her chest as he *totally ignored her* and reached for his bag. He put it on the bed and *started to pack*? She couldn't believe it.

He emptied a drawer. "There's a flight from San Francisco in ninety minutes. I just have to get to the local—" He looked up, catching her eye; it was, she was certain, glittery cold. "Look, I know how you feel," he stammered. "I really do. And I wouldn't even dream of suggesting it, Doris, if you weren't a mother and you didn't understand. I mean, I wouldn't ever think of leaving like this, I mean if this *crisis* hadn't come up. Oh, it's not just the tooth fairy—the thing is, she could have *swallowed* the tooth. It could be lodged God knows where! Now, I know this leaves you a bit—uh—at loose ends, but there's no reason for you to leave too. The room's paid for. Anyway, I'm probably doing you a favor. If I stayed I wouldn't be wonderful company. Listen, did you happen to see my hairbrush?"

She saw his hairbrush. It was on the sofa. It was in her hand. It was hurling through the air, aimed neatly at his head.

It crashed against the wall.

He gave it a long, incredulous look. He saved the look and threw it at Doris. Then he nodded. "You're feeling a little rejected, right? Well, I can understand that, believe me, but I want you to know my leaving has nothing to do with us."

She glared at him.

"Doris, Doris. This is an emergency! I have a *sick child* at home!"

"Oh will you stop that!" Doris exploded. "It's got nothing to do with the goddamn tooth fairy! You're consumed with guilt and the only way you can deal with it is by getting as far away from me as possible!"

"Okay! Guilty! I plead guilty to feeling guilty. Is that so strange? Doris, don't you understand? We're *cheating*! Once a year we lie to our families and sneak off to a hotel in California and commit adultery!—not that I want to stop doing it—but yes, I feel guilt. I admit it."

"*Admit* it? Sweet Jesus. You take out ads. You probably stop strangers in the street! It's a wonder you haven't hired a *skywriter*! I'm amazed you haven't had a scarlet *A* embroidered on your shorts. You think that by *talking* about it, by wringing your hands and beating your breast, it will somehow give you divine absolution. So you wander around like—like an open nerve, saying, 'I'm cheating, but look how *guilty* I feel, so I must really be a nice guy!' And to top it all, you have the incredible arrogance to think you're the only one in the world with a conscience. Well that doesn't make you a nice guy. You know what that makes you? A *horse's ass*!"

They stared at each other.

He rubbed his jaw. "You know something?" he said slowly. "I liked you better *before* you started reading."

"Mmm. Well, that's not why you're leaving, George."

"Doris, it's not the end of the world. I'm not leaving you permanently. Look, we'll see each other next year."

With a sinking feeling, she shook her head. "No," she said quietly, "I don't think you will."

"Come on. You don't mean that."

She nodded. "I mean that."

"Come on. You don't mean that." He threw up his hands. "You mean, just because I have to leave a little bit early on one occasion, you're willing to throw away a lifetime of weekends? I can't *believe* it."

"Believe it."

"I can't." He reached for his shoes. "Listen, we'll talk about it in the car."

"In the *car*?"

"I couldn't get a Hertz at the airport. I took a taxi. I need a lift."

She was shaking her head. "You take the cake."

"No," he said, "I'll leave it for you. I know you like chocolate."

She glared at him briefly, and stalked from the room.

He finished packing. He'd never seen her *acting* like this before. He'd thought she was soft, sweet, understanding. Well . . . she wasn't. She was turning hard. Did he really need more *demands* in his life? The thing that he'd loved about Doris to begin with

She walked to the lot. She'd seen him acting like this before, but she'd thought he'd grown out of it. Well . . . he hadn't. He was such a baby. Did she really need another baby in her life? The thing that she'd loved about George to begin with was

was the fact that she'd been so even-tempered, so undemanding, so *cheerful* about it. If he wanted more hairbrushes thrown at his head, he didn't have to travel three thousand miles. That kind of crap he could get at home.

He locked up his bags and looked at the room. *Happy 5th Anniversary, Darling*. Well, he nodded, that was that. And it wasn't five years. It was only five nights. . . .What could a woman rightfully expect of a man she'd only spent *five nights* with? God. The pain in his stomach was worse. Probably an ulcer.

He ate some cake; it tasted dry.

And besides, it clearly meant nothing to her, or she couldn't toss it away like this. After five *years*!

Women—he ate some more of the cake—Women—he picked up his coat and bag—were totally cold and devoid of logic.

He stalked to the car.

the fact that he'd been so sweet and romantic, such fun to be with. Was *this* any fun? This was absurd! If she wanted the tooth fairy routing her dreams, she didn't have to travel two hundred miles. There were plenty of loose molars at home.

She pulled out the keys and opened the car. What really got her—she sat at the wheel—what really got her was how very little the whole thing meant—to him. This weekend she'd thought of all year, and *he* could just recklessly toss it away. Which not only made her cheap, but a fool! A terrible fool.

She lit up a Kent, from the wrong end.

She'd really thought it was more than sex, but clearly, men couldn't think beyond sex. Or maybe they couldn't *feel* beyond sex.

Men—she stubbed out the smelly smoke—Men—she turned the ignition key—were totally cold and devoid of emotion.

She started the car.

He slammed the door and lit a cigarette. "I can't believe you can be so casual."

"I don't see any point in going on."

"Oh no," he snapped. "Don't do that to me. Don't play blackmail games with me, Doris. That's not what our relationship's all about."

"What *is* it about?" She pulled the car from the lot to the road.

"You don't know?" he asked her dryly.

"Yes. I know. But it seems to be different from what *you* know. We have different ideas of what it's about, and that's why I think we should just break it off."

"My God. You really *are* serious."

"I've always been serious."

"You've always been *fun*."

"Well, it's hard to be *fun* with a man who's bleeding all over the rug. Pardon me, I shouldn't have mentioned blood. I know you're delicate."

"Doris I've got a *commitment* there."

"Right," she said slowly. "And you don't have one here?"

"Here? I thought our only commitment was just to show up."

"Oh. I see. Nice and tidy. Just two, friendly sexual partners who meet once a year, touch, and let go."

"Right—I mean, make a right turn here. I don't know, I don't know, I don't know, Doris. Maybe I was only kidding myself. I mean . . . I'm human."

"Well, so am I." She made the turn.

"No you're not. I mean, you're different. You've always been stronger. More able to . . . cope."

"*Cope?"* She closed her eyes for a second; she opened them quickly and stared at the road. When she spoke again, her voice was level. "Cope," she said, and nodded slowly. "During the past year I picked up the phone and started to call you a dozen times. I couldn't seem to stop thinking about you. You kept slipping over into my 'real life' and it scared hell out of me. More to the point, I felt *guilty*. So I decided to stop seeing you." She looked at him quickly with the side of her eyes. He was looking sober. She looked at the road. The sign said Mendocino Airport. She kept going. "At first I wasn't going to show up at all, but then I thought that wouldn't be fair, that at least I owed you an explanation. So . . . I came." She turned up the ramp. "And then . . . then you walked in the door of the cottage, I knew I couldn't do it. That no matter what the price, I was willing to pay it."

She parked.

He was sitting there, holding his head. "Oh, God. I feel so *guilty*," he anguished.

"I know. You'd better go home, George." She leaned across him and opened the door.

A skycap hustled the bag from his lap, and started away. Rising slowly, George followed.

Doris just sat in the car for a while, the door still open. She lit a cigarette. She was feeling numb. She watched as he disappeared through the door. Beyond, on the runway, she looked at the plane. A small plane. She could see its nose with the single propeller. She watched the propeller starting to spin. The plane took off. She watched it soaring over the car. She tossed the cigarette out the window. All she felt was . . . nothing at all. A little like being dead, only worse.

"I love you, Doris."

She turned, slowly. George was poking his head through the door. She saw him through a terrible mist in her eyes.

"I love you," he repeated. "I'm an idiot, I suspect I'm deeply neurotic, and I'm no bargain—but I do love you." He cocked his head. "Will you let me stay?"

She reached for his hand; he moved to the seat and into her arms.

"Doris," he whispered, kissing her, "Doris, oh Doris, what the hell are we going to do?"

"Touch," she said. "Touch and hold on very tight—until tomorrow."

She started the car.

memo from

G. Peters, Tax Consultant

Westport, Conn.

date 2/24/61

Harry's Mother's 10th Birthday!!

EIGHT

At 10:30 on Friday morning, George walked out of his Westport office, carrying with him a Gucci bag. He quickly walked down the quiet block, hurrying southward to pick up his car. A horn-honk blasted the morning air.

Honk! "George?"

George looked up. His mother-in-law was parked at the curb, revving the motor and pounding the horn of a silver Mercedes 220-S. George walked up to the shiny car. Mrs. Wynant did not smile.

George smiled. "Hello—Carol," George said slowly, still not used to calling her "Mother," his own mother having been a plain gray lady of ample bosom and tender smile, who got out of her cheerful, calico apron exactly twice in her calico life, once to attend his father's funeral, and once, at last, to attend her own. The notion that one could have a slim blond Mommy who drove a Mercedes and a series of husbands to the brink of despair was a fact he could never quite take in his stride.

"Well! I'm delighted I caught you, George."

"Well, you didn't exactly catch me, Carol." He made a flashy show of his bag and his teeth. "What I mean is, I'm catching a copter in twenty minutes and—"

"Caught is caught," Mrs. Wynant announced. "I'll drive you to the airport. Open the door."

"It's only the local airport," he sputtered, "and it's really—" he looked at her businesslike eyes and nodded slowly. "Caught is caught." He opened the door.

She pulled from the curb.

They drove in silence for half a second.

"You've been working late every night for a month," she began negotiations.

"Right," George said. "Someone has to pay for the sudden influx of pillbox hats. Boy, there's one thing I'll say for Nixon—nobody wanted to look like his wife."

"You're avoiding the issue."

"What's the issue?"

"George," she flicked him an icy look, "I want to get down to brass tacks."

"Carol, I've been getting down to *income* tax. It's *busy* season."

"That wasn't the question."

"But's that's the answer."

"The question is, why are you leaving Helen?"

"I'm *not* 'leaving Helen.' " He looked out the window. "How the hell did you come up with that?"

"Mmm." She tapped her nails on the wheel. "A connection I make with baggage and airports and the fact that I don't see Helen in the car." She was chewing her lip. "Are you planning to meet her at the airport, George?"

"Carol, you know that Helen's at home."

"Then logic would have it, you're leaving Helen."

He tilted his head. "You sure you're not a Russian trial lawyer?"

"Are you trying to call me a Communist, George?"

"Right. You're the only Red in the country who said on the day that Havana fell, 'Drat! Now the nearest roulette's in San Juan!' " George made a wink. "You gorgeous sneak."

"Mmm. You fail to amuse me, George."

"Well, it's a failing I've learned to live with. Listen, I'm going on a business trip, Carol. I go every year."

"Are you sure you're not running away from the problem?"

"Of course I'm not running away from the problem." He looked at her quickly. "*What* problem?"

"Let's call it . . . another of your failings, George."

"And what does *that* mean?"

"Do you want it spelled out?"

"Yes! I'd like to know what the—"

"I-M-P-"

"Oh."

"T-E-N-T."

"Great. You win the spelling bee. Congratulations." George felt himself turning crimson and hot. He was standing, naked, in Yankee Stadium, while ten thousand people sniggered and stomped and the umpire called, '*no balls, no strikes.*' "Terrific," he said, and stared out the window, "How did you manage to find this out?"

"Let's say Helen dropped a few hints."

"What *kind* of 'hints'?"

"Well, she snapped at me this morning and I said, My goodness, Helen, you're edgy, and then I noticed a pimple on her chin."

"*What*?"

"My daughter does not get pimples. Not without help. So I said to her, Helen—how's your sex life?"

"And what did she say?"

"Nothing."

"Oh."

"Have you seen a doctor?"

George winced. "Listen, Carol—I just don't think this is any of your—"

"Listen, George—when my daughter gets pimples at thirty-seven, I *assure* you it's my—"

"All right. All right. All *right*. I saw a doctor."

"And what did he say?"

"Oh Christ." George sighed, and wondered why the airport was so far away. At the next civic meeting he'd introduce a bill to move it in closer. He lit a cigarette. "Not much. He said it was no big deal."

"Mmm. That seems to summarize the problem. The question is, did he have a cure? I mean, did he tell you you'd *caught* it in time?"

"What do you mean—*caught* it in time? Carol, it's a slight reflex problem. It's not a progressive, terminal disease!"

"George, you don't have to get so upset."

"How would you feel if we discussed your frigidity?"

"La!" she chuckled and steered up a ramp. "I assure you, dear, I didn't get three husbands by being frigid."

"I know. I just figured that's how you lost them."

"Sticks and stones." She chuckled again. "But that doesn't answer our problem, does it?"

"*Our* problem?"

"All right. If you insist then, Helen's problem. Have you thought about seeing a specialist, George?"

"You mean a dermatologist for Helen's chin?"

Thankfully, the car pulled up to the terminal. George stubbed his smoke out and picked up his bag.

"As a matter of fact," he said very firmly, "the problem will be gone by the time I get back."

She doubted him sternly under very blond brows. "How can you know that?"

"Look, I just *know*." He opened the door. "I can *feel* it, okay?" He studied her doubt. "Because," he exploded, "when I get to California, I'm seeing an *expert*! Bye-bye, Carol." He got to his feet, hoisted his luggage, and turned around.

George closed the door.

NINE

George checked his watch (12:55) and switched on the radio exactly in time for the 6:30 news, or at least the commercial at 6:31. A female vocalist sang, "It's Pepsi—For Those Who Think Young." George looked around. The cottage hadn't changed. The couch had the same brown-flowered chintz, the piano had the same cloisonné vase, the bed had the same shiny-brass frame, and the chair had the same little cigarette burn that he himself had personally made in 1958. Or was it '59?

He opened his bag.

In Cucamonga
They're thinkin' younga
And it's Pepsi—
For Those Who Think Young!
Yeah!

And now, Ron Dobbs with the KFX news. . . .

For a moment, George mentally tuned out the news and was stuck with the thought of *For Those Who Think Young*. The thing was to get his thing to think young—or at least, Positive. He thought of *The Power Of Positive Thinking*. He thought about other inspiring

Doris drove through a pocket of static, which left her with the echo of *Those Who Think Young*. God only knew she was thinking young—and God only knew what George would think. She was certain their relationship was deeper than sex, but what if it wasn't? She'd spent the books. *Sunrise at Campobello . . . The Little Engine That Could . . .* He thought of *The Sun Also Rises.* He groaned. He started unpacking his Sulka robe, his blue pajamas, his Trojan pack. He hung up his new Meladandri jacket and took off his Turnbull & Asser shirt. He retired to the bathroom, showered quickly, shaved neatly, and slapped his face with Zizanie. Now . . . he studied himself. Not too bad. Not Porfirio Rubirosa, but nothing like Truman Capote either. It would be all right. It really would. Everything would turn out perfectly fine.

"*. . . that Americans are training six thousand Cubans, both here and abroad, to execute the liberation of Cuba. Elsewhere, President Kennedy stated, the U. S. would not be provoked into action in Southeast Asia.*"

He brushed his teeth for the second time, smiled at the mirror (like Gregory Peck?), and practiced saying, "Hi, Lover," "Hey, baby," "Hi, babe. . . ."

morning in terrible doubt. She'd taken a serious look at herself and burst out laughing; that was before she'd burst into tears, which made her look even worse than before. Last year she'd weighed 112 and he'd called her his Dream Girl. Very nice. This year she weighed 140 and could only be a Dream Girl for Captain Ahab. Well, what the hell. It would be a test. It would be all right. It really would. Everything would turn out perfectly fine. The radio crackled:

"*. . . that Americans are training six thousand Cubans, both here and abroad, to execute the liberation of Cuba. Elsewhere, President Kennedy stated, the U. S. would not be provoked into action in Southeast Asia.*"

She parked in the lot of the Sea Shadows Inn, and clicked off the radio, checking her face in the rear-view mirror.

Oh, what the hell . . .

The door slammed, and Doris called, "George?"

He flashed himself a final (Bogart?) smile, "Be right

out, baby," and entered the room. She was facing the fireplace, warming her hands. He tightened the sash of his blue silk robe, and lowered his voice to a husky (yet terribly tender) bark. "How are ya, Lover?"

She turned, smiling.

He paled, frowning.

For a long moment he stared, frozen, trying to figure out—Mother of God—she was *four hundred and twelve months pregnant.*

She grinned at him foolishly. "Guess what?"

Mute, he backed himself to the wall.

"I know," she nodded and held up a hand, "I know. You've heard of middle-aged spread, but this is ridiculous."

"Jesus Christ! Doris, what have you *done* to yourself?"

She shrugged. "Well I can't take *all* the credit."

His breath came whistling out in a burst, like the hissing sound of a punctured dream. He continued to stare.

"Honey?" she said. "When you haven't seen an old friend in a year, isn't it usual to kiss them hello?"

"What?" He nodded, mesmerized. "Sure. Sure." He moved to her, very slowly, steering a course to her starboard side, and kissed her, very lightly, on the cheek. "Pregnant," he muttered. "Pregnant, pregnant." Shaking his head, he paced to the couch.

"Hey," she was saying, "you okay, pal?"

"Fine! I'm just—a little—surprised."

"*You're* surprised." She rubbed at her back. "I insisted on visiting the dead rabbit's grave."

She laughed.

He didn't.

He stared at her numbly. If you didn't count the body, she looked okay. Her hair was back to its natural color, and longer, and her face looked exactly like Doris. Except that *Doris* wouldn't *do* this to him. He started pacing. He was getting mad.

"How come you're wearing your robe and pajamas," she said, "when it's only seven o'clock?"

"Why the hell do you think?" he snapped. "I'm rehearsing a Noel Coward play!"

"Oh."

He flung himself at the couch and, scowling, watched as she sat in a chair, kicking her shoes off, rubbing her feet.

"George?" she said slowly, "is there something on your mind?"

"Not any more." He got up to pace. "My God. You have to be eight months pregnant."

She smiled. "Exactly," she said and looked in his eyes. "Honey, it isn't all that tragic. We'll just—have to figure out some other way to communicate."

"Great! You got any ideas?"

"Well . . . we could talk?"

"*Talk? Talk* I can get at home."

"Well . . . sex *I* can get at home." She grinned and then said from the side of her mouth, "And as you can see, that ain't just talk."

"Oh really?" He whirled. "And what the hell's that supposed to make *me*?"

"George, what *is* the matter with you?"

"Matter? I'll tell you what's the matter with me. I'm the only man in America who's just kept an illicit assignation with a woman who looks like a frigate in full sail. And then she asks me what's the matter."

"There's something else. You're not yourself."

"Let me be the judge of who I am."

"Why are you so angry, George?"

"What was that crack about sex at home? Is that supposed to reflect on me? You don't think I have normal sex drives or something?"

"Of course I think you have normal sex drives. I just meant I look forward to seeing you for a lot of other reasons *aside* from sex. George—could we have lasted for ten years if that's all we had in common?" She looked a little worried. "Could we, George?"

He smiled at her. "No. Of course not, Doris."

"We're friends as well as lovers, aren't we?"

"We are." He was starting to feel like a louse. "I'm

sorry, Doris. Jesus. Forgive me. You drive all the way up here in your condition, and then I behave like a ridiculous idiot. You should have thrown something at me. Really. I'm sorry." He opened his suitcase and took out some Scotch. "You want some?"

"I'd love it. But my stomach would hate it."

"Right." He poured himself a very stiff drink.

"What's bothering you, George?"

"Nothing." He drank. "It's just that I was looking forward to . . . an intimate weekend." He put down the bottle and prowled, with his glass.

"And you think we can only be intimate through sex."

"Well let's put it this way: I sure think it helps."

"Oh, maybe," she said. "At the beginning."

"At the beginning?"

"Well . . ." she sat there, massaging her back, "it seems to me, every year when we meet, it's always a little bit awkward at first . . . but we usually solve it with a lot of heavy breathing between the sheets."

"Honey," he said, "if we're not gonna breathe heavily, would you mind not discussing it?"

"Look, I just meant that—maybe we need something else to break the ice."

He picked up the bottle and poured another shot. "I'm wide open to suggestions."

"So how about this? Suppose I tell you something secret about myself that I've never told anyone else in my life."

"I think I've had enough surprises for today." He moved to the fireplace and stared at the fire.

"But this one, you'll like. George? I've been having these sex dreams about you."

He turned, suddenly. "When?"

"Just lately." She grinned. "Almost every night. They're really strange. They're always the same. We're making love but it's always under water. In caves, grottoes, swimming pools—but always under water. Isn't that weird?" She lifted her shoulders. "Probably something to do with being pregnant."

He nodded thoughtfully. "Under water, huh?"

"Uh-huh. So now tell me *your* dark secret."

He nodded thoughtfully. "I can't swim."

She burst out laughing. "*Literally,* George?"

"Of course, literally. When I tell you I can't swim, I mean I can't swim."

"How in the world could you not swim?"

"Well . . . I just never learned as a kid. But I never told anybody—well, Helen found out when she pushed me off a dock and I almost drowned. But the kids don't even know. When we go to the beach I pretend I'm having trouble with my trick knee."

"You have a trick knee."

"No. They don't know that either."

"You see? It's working. I mean, we're talking like two people who've already been to bed." She smiled, and pushed herself up from the chair.

He looked at her. "Something I can get you?" he said.

"You want to change bodies for half an hour?"

"Hey, look—you want to go for a walk or something? Get some fresh air?"

"Is there something wrong with the air in here?"

"Yeah. It reeks of unused bed." He sighed. "If you wait a second, I'll just slip out of something comfortable."

"Oh . . . Okay, honey. Whatever you say. It's the least I can do for you."

He nodded. "You said it."

"You folks want some Irish coffee or something?" Chalmers said as they walked through the garden. "It's nippy out here." He was sitting alone at a redwood table, reading a copy of *Doctor No.*

"Thanks," Doris said, "but my doctor said no."

"Mmm." Chalmers seemed to eye her abstractedly. He nodded, turned, and then looked up at George. "How about you? I got some right here." He lifted a thermos.

Chalmers appeared a lot older, George thought; his hair was all white, but it wasn't just that.

"Thanks," George said, "I think I could use it." He opened the thermos, filling its cup. "To better luck next time." He looked at Doris.

"And how's *Mrs*. Chalmers?" Doris said quickly.

Chalmers looked up. "She died," he said flatly.

"Oh . . . I'm *sorry*."

"Yeah . . . Well . . ." He was trying to look for something to add; he couldn't find it. "Yeah," he finished.

George said, "And Larry. How's he doing?"

"Oh." Chalmers nodded. "Doin' just fine. Bought himself a bar down in San Diego. Had twins."

"Hey that's wonderful," Doris said. "Do you visit him often?"

"Well . . . he's busy, you know . . ."

"Mr. Chalmers," George said suddenly. "We were thinking of going to the movies tonight. *The Apartment*'s in town. Have you seen it?"

"Nope. Sorry. Can't give you a recommendation."

"Well, what I mean—would you like to see it? I mean, come with us? It's supposed to be good."

"Oh . . ." Chalmers smiled. "Well . . . maybe . . . . Maybe that'd be nice. We'll see . . ."

Doris stretched up and kissed George's ear.

"What's that for?"

"Being nice. Asking Chalmers to go to the movies."

"I just figured it might take two of us to navigate you into the seat of a car."

Doris sighed, and leaned her back up against a tree. "Someday before you're old and gray, you will learn to take a compliment by just saying thank you."

"Don't look now, but I'm old and gray."

"Stop it, George. You're thirty-seven."

"You want to sit down? This bench seems to offer a view of the pond."

They sat. He tossed a pebble at the pond. In the twilight, the ground was chirring with crickets. He lit a cigarette. She was watching him closely.

"You want to tell me about it?" she said.

He stared at the pond. There were seven swans. A-swimming. And two ducks. "Tell you what?"

"What's on your mind."

"Oh." He tossed his cigarette at the pond. "Okay," he decided. "I might as well get it out in the open. I mean, it's nothing to be ashamed of. It's very simple, really, it's"—he considered jumping in the pond and drowning—"it's—my sex life."

"Your sex life?"

He nodded. "Lately"—the pond would be three feet deep and he'd just get wet and get double pneumonia—"lately"—he plunged—"lately—Helen's lost her interest in sex, is what it is. Oh, she tries. God knows, she tries. But I can tell she's just going through the motions, you know?"

"Oh . . . Gee . . . Do you know what's causing it, George?"

He shrugged. "Well, Helen's always had a lot of hang-ups about sex. For one thing, she always thought of it as just a healthy, normal, pleasant . . . sport." He looked at her. "Don't you think that's twisted?"

"Only if you're Catholic."

"Yeah. Right. You're joking," he said. "But there's really a lot to be said for guilt. I mean, if you don't feel guilty about it, I really think you're missing half of the fun. To Helen, sex has always been good, clean . . . *entertainment*. I mean, no wonder she got bored with it, you know?" He looked at Doris. She didn't seem to know. "Anyway," he barged on, "for some reason, my sex drive has increased while hers has—" he pushed his thumb towards the ground.

She looked at his thumb.

He hid it in his hand.

"Gee, that's funny." She nodded slowly. "It's usually just the other way around."

"Are you accusing me of lying?" he snapped.

"Of course not." She was looking at him curiously now. "George, why are you so edgy today?"

"Because I think it's unfair to talk about Helen behind her back. I mean, she's not here to defend herself."

"Oh," Doris said. "Well . . . we'll just count it as The Bad Story."

"About Helen?"

She nodded.

George shook his head. "Actually, that wasn't the bad story. I mean, she can't *help* that . . . you know?" He really felt like a cur. "But I'll tell you the good story."

"Hey. You've never done *that* before. I mean—started with the good story. You must be softening."

"Doris, do you mind? Where was I? Oh, yeah. In London. We were checking into a hotel in London and there was a man in a formal coat and striped trousers standing at the front entrance. Helen handed him her suitcase and sailed on into the lobby. The man followed her and very politely pointed out that not only didn't he work at the hotel but that he was the Danish ambassador. Without batting an eye, she said, 'Well, that's marvelous. Maybe you can tell us the good places to eat in Copenhagen'—and he did! The point is that it doesn't seem to bother her when she makes a total ass of herself. I really admire that."

"And what is it you don't admire?"

"Her damned sense of humor!"

"Oh good," Doris giggled. "Those are the stories I like the best."

"All right," he said, "Well, we—" George got up and started to pace. There was still time to switch. He could tell her the one about What Helen Said When He Ran Out Of Gas On The Merritt Parkway. Or the famous Washing-The-Dog story. He chain-lit a cigarette. "We'd come home from a party and we'd had a frew drinks and we went to bed and we started to make love. Well . . . nothing happened—for me—I couldn't—well, you get the idea. It was no big deal. We laughed about it." He took in a deep lungful of smoke. "Then about half an hour later, just as I was falling off to sleep, she said, 'It's funny, when I married a C.P.A., I always thought it would be his *eyes* that would go first." George kept his eyes on the smoke he'd exhaled. After a while, he looked up at Doris. She wasn't laughing. She was just sitting there looking pregnant and Sweet.

"She was just trying to make you feel better, honey."

"Swell. Well, it didn't. Some things aren't funny." He studied his cigarette again. "I suppose what I'm trying to say is that the thing that bugs me the most about Helen is simply the fact that she broke my pecker!" He flicked the damn cigarette out at the pond.

"You're . . . impotent?" Doris said very gently, from behind him.

"Slightly." He turned to face her and shrugged. "Okay. Now *five* people know. Me, you, Helen and her mother."

"Who's the fifth?"

"Chet Huntley." He gritted his teeth. "I'm sure her mother gave him the bulletin for the six o'clock news." Pounding his fist, he started to pace. He checked Doris. She still wasn't laughing. On the other hand, her lip wasn't curled in contempt; she hadn't turned pale, nasty, or away. She was just sitting there looking pregnant and Kind.

"When did it happen, honey?" she said.

"*Happen?*" He wheeled on her. "Doris, we're not talking about a freeway accident! I mean you don't wake up one morning and say, 'Oh shoot, the old family jewels have gone on the blink.' It's a gradual thing."

"And you really blame Helen?"

"Of course not." He started pacing again. "I—I wanted to tell you but I just couldn't think of a graceful way of working it into the conversation." He laughed, harshly. "To tell you the truth I was just waiting for you to say, 'What's new?' and I was gonna say, 'Nothing, but I'll tell you what's old.' "

"Oh darling."

"Oh shit." He continued to pace. The sky had gone dark.

"How's Helen reacting?"

"I don't know. We haven't discussed it much, but I get the feeling she regards it as a lapse in one's social responsibility. You know, rather like letting your partner down in tennis by not holding your serve. Christ!"

"Is there . . . anything I can say that will help?"

"Say anything you want except 'it's all in your head.' I mean, I'm no doctor, but I have a great sense of direction." He lit another cigarette. He was sick of lighting another cigarette. He stamped it out. "Look," he said, "to tell you the truth, I'm not too crazy about the whole subject. Let's forget it, huh?" She was still looking Sweet, Kind . . . and pregnant. "Seriously, Doris. I'll be okay. The patient's not dead yet—just resting."

She extended her hand.

"Doris, that statement hardly calls for congratulations."

"I know. I just need help getting up."

"You want to go in?"

"It's kind of chilly."

"Yeah." He helped her up to her feet. She smiled. He smiled. He felt very close to her. Then he remembered that he always had.

"God!" She suddenly twisted away.

"What's the matter?"

"Wow!" She was holding her stomach. "It's okay now. The baby just kicked."

"Yeah? What's he got to kick about? He'll never have it this good in his life. Come on, let's go in."

"Funny," she said, as they walked through the garden. "He hasn't kicked me in quite a while."

"Well, maybe he was trying to kick me." George kicked a stone. "Everyone else has been taking a shot. Why not him?"

"Funny," she said.

"You want some . . . warm milk or something?"

Shaking her head, she sat on the couch. "That's the most depressing part about being pregnant. People always offer you warm milk." She was rubbing her back again. "Oh, boy. That Ethel Kennedy must really love kids."

He stoked the fire. "How do you feel about being pregnant?"

"Mmm. Catatonic, incredulous, angry, pragmatic, and finally maternal. Pretty much in that order."

"Your vocabulary's improving." He smiled and poured himself a Scotch.

"Give me one puff of a cigarette and I'll tell you how come."

"You can have a whole cigarette."

"Listen, even a puff'll make me dizzy."

"Then you can't have a puff. Why don't you lie down or something?"

"One puff." She pulled up her feet and squirmed to a lying position on the couch.

"We'll compromise. I'll blow some at you." He lit a cigarette, and sat on the arm of the couch by her head. He blew some smoke at her. "Now, how come your vocabulary's better?"

"Well," she smiled, inhaling his smoke, "see, I was confined to bed for the first three months of my pregnancy? So rather than it being a total loss, I took a correspondence course. Blow some more smoke."

"You're something, you know? That's—marvelous, honey."

"Mmm. There's a kind of ironic twist to it, too. I didn't graduate from high school the first time because I got pregnant. And now I did graduate from high school"—she tapped her stomach "—because I got pregnant."

He laughed. "I didn't know you had a sense of order."

"Aw, that's unfair. I'm much better at housework now. Must be the nesting instinct. Anyway, the day my diploma came in the mail, Harry bought me a corsage and took me out dancing. Well, we didn't really dance—we lumbered. Afterwards, we went to a malt shop and had a hot fudge sundae. That's my nice story about him."

"He still selling real estate?"

"Why are you putting your cigarette out?"

"When did you start smoking?"

"Oh George. I've been smoking for years. I'll tell you exactly when I started to smoke. In this very room in nineteen fifty-five on the day we discovered I could have gotten pregnant.

"Oh. Yeah. That was pretty scary."

"Oh, it wasn't then. It was after that. When you were trying to figure out how you could put the obstetrician bills on *your* Blue Cross, so Harry wouldn't have to know I was pregnant."

"Yeah. Well. I got carried away."

"I know. I've decided I love that about you, and in answer to your question, he's not selling real estate he's selling insurance. He likes it. Gives him a chance to look up his old army buddies. . . . How's Michael?"

George got up and threw another log on the dwindling fire. "Michael," he said, "is doing terrific. In fact, I now know two high school graduates. He finished early, in January. Got accepted to Harvard. Then we had a big fight because he said he didn't want to go to college. He said colleges are factories that manufacture brains and he didn't want to have a mass-produced head. Then he said, 'Besides, I'm just sick of being a kid.' So I said, 'You think *that's* sickening, try having to be an adult for a while.' Anyway, we compromised. I told him he could take a job for a year, figuring he'd get some terrible job he'd be happy to quit. So right away he got a job as a New York reporter for the Associated Press."

"Oh George, that's wonderful. I'm so *proud* of him."

"Yeah." He looked at her lying on the couch. She had a pillow stuck under the small of her back, and her legs were tucked at a peculiar angle. "Doris, are you comfortable in that position?"

She laughed. "My dear, when you're in my condition you're not comfortable in any position."

"Come on. Why don't you get on the bed. At least you can spread out."

"Hmm. As it were. You think you could help me up?"

"Yeah, I think I could manage that." He moved to help her. "How did you twist your feet around like that?"

"I don't know. I haven't seen them in almost a year."

He untwisted her feet. "Listen, while I'm here shall I send them your regards?"

She laughed, and he reached for her arms to pull her up. And then something absolutely terrible happened.

It wasn't only Doris who started to rise.

George made a strangled sound in his throat. He got her to her feet and then stared at her.

"George? Why are you looking at me like that?"

"I'm not," he said quickly, "I'm not looking at you." To prove it, he looked directly at the ceiling and then at the piano with the Scotch bottle on it, for which he headed. "So tell me another story about Harry."

"I had trouble telling him I was pregnant and when I finally did he looked at me and—George, why are you *looking* at me like that?"

There was absolutely no doubt about it now. The old gibber was back in the game. He put down the glass. "It's obscene!" he exploded.

"What's obscene?"

"When I touched you, I started to get excited! Oh, my God." He started to pace. "I mean, what kind of a pervert am I? I'm staring at a two-hundred-pound pregnant woman and I'm getting hot! Just the *sight* of you is making me excited! Oh God!"

"Oh, darling." She was grinning, ear to ear. "Let me tell you something. That's the nicest thing anyone has said to me in months."

"It's not funny, Doris."

"Aren't you pleased?"

"Pleased? I feel like I did on my seventh birthday. My uncle gave me fifty cents. I ran two miles and when I got there, the candy store was closed."

"But honey, doesn't this solve your problem?"

"Doris, the idea doesn't solve a thing. It's the execution that counts."

She giggled. "I really got to you, huh?"

"And there's only one thing I can do about it now—Excuse me." He marched to the piano and sat and launched into Chopin's Revolutionary Étude. He closed his eyes and played with the piano.

"That's marvelous, George. My God, you're incredible!"

"Yeah. Incredible." He kept on playing. She looked at him, awestruck. George looked away. He kept on playing.

"George, you're—are you really as good as I *think* you are?"

"How good do you think I am?"

"Sensational!"

"Then I'm not as good as you think I am." He continued to play.

"I don't understand it! That piano's been sitting there for ten years and you've hardly touched it. Why today?"

"Beats a cold shower." He continued to play.

"You play to release sexual tension?"

"You don't get this good without a lot of practice."

"Wow!" she said. "You're full of surprises."

"Yeah. I know. You live with a man for ten days and you never really know him."

"Why didn't you tell me?"

"Hell. I had other ways to entertain you." He continued to play.

"Mmm. I always knew you had wonderful hands—"

"Listen, lady. I only work here. I'm not allowed to date the customers."

She moved away.

He didn't feel better. He started pounding out the second movement.

"George? You still feel—"

"Yeah." He nodded. "I have a feeling it'll take all six Brandenberg Concertos."

"George, you'll be *exhausted*."

"That's the idea."

"Mmm. Well I have a better idea." She was holding out her hand. "C'mere."

He stopped playing.

"Come on." She was crooking her finger at him.

He stood up slowly.

"Come on," she said, and took him by the hand; she was starting to lead him to the bed.

"Doris?" He looked at her doubtfully.

"It's all right," she said. "It'll be okay."

"But you can't—"

"I know. We'll work something out." And standing by the bed, she kissed him, tenderly, and then, hungrily, and then he made a furry growl in his throat and grabbed her, tightly, and all of a sudden she pulled away with a terrible yelp. She was doubled over.

"Doris, what is it?"

For an answer, she screwed up her face and moaned.

"Doris. For God's sake. What *is* it?"

For answer, she stopped moaning, and stared.

"Doris?"

"If . . . memory serves me correctly . . . I just had a labor pain. Excuse me." She sat down slowly on the bed.

George stood very, very still. He was trying to absorb this information, but it kept on seeping out through his mouth in a series of sounds like, "No, no, no. No," he said. "Maybe it's indigestion."

"No," she said. "Indigestion's different. For one thing, it doesn't make your eyes bug out."

"But you *can't* be in labor. You said you were only eight months pregnant!" He stared her again, and then covered his eyes. "Oh my God. What have I *done*?"

"What have *you* done?"

"I brought it on. It was my—selfishness." He started to pace.

"George, don't be stupid. You had nothing to do with it."

"God. Don't treat me like a *child*, Doris."

"George, will you stop getting so excited?"

"*Excited?* My God! I thought I had trouble with my sex life *before*. Can you imagine what *this*'ll do it it? God!"

"George, will you ju—oh! *Oh*!OoooooooooooooooooooooooooooooOOOOOOOOOOO*wow*—I think I better lie down."

"Jesus, what kind of a man am I? What kind of man would *do* such a thing?"

"George . . . may I *say* something?"

"Look, I appreciate what you're trying to do, but nothing you can say will make me feel better."

"George, I'm not trying to make you feel better. I'm having a baby."

He turned. "I know that. What do you think I'm—"

"George. I mean now."

He'd thought she'd said "now." She didn't say "now." "You didn't say 'now.' "

"George, I said 'now.' "

"No."

"I have a history of short labor."

"No."

"George, could you just go-oh-oh-oh-oh-oh-oh-oh-OH-oh-oh-oh-oh to the phone and find out where the nearest hospital is?"

"No!"

"*No?*"

"No! You don't want to go to a hospital. It's a false alarm. It *has* to be a false alarm."

"Honey, just try and get a hold of yourself. And a doctor. George—like it or not, I'm gonna have a baby."

"You *can't* have a baby. We're not married!"

"*What?*"

"I mean, it's gonna look—odd."

"George—OH!" She got to her feet with more speed than he'd dreamt she could muster.

"Where are you going?"

"The bathroom."

"Why?"

"I don't have time to answer you noooooOOOOWW-oh!"

She was out of the room. For a moment he stood there, totally frozen. Terror shot him over to the phone. Stark panic dialed an *O*.

Chalmers answered on the second ring.

"Mr. Chalmers, where's the nearest hospital?

"George? Is something the matter?"

"*No!*" George said. "It's just—well it's just—it's my fr—uh—lov—uh—Dor—uh—mist—uh—wi—uh—WIFE! It's my wife!"

"Is she sick?"

"*No!* It's just—something unexpected came up. She got pregnant. And now she's gonna have a baby."

"Now?"

"Now."

"It's seventy miles."

"Seventy miles? Oh my God. Look, just get them on the phone for me, will you?"

"Hold on."

"Yeah. Right." George cupped the phone. "Doris? You okay?"

No answer, and he felt the blood rush out of his head.

"Doris? Oh, Doris!" He dropped the phone and started to run.

"Stay out! I'm just—busy."

"Oh. Oh God." He ran back to the phone in time to hear a switchboard operator answer, "La Riorita Hospital."

"Emergency—uh—Maternity!"

"Which do you want, sir?"

"Emergency Maternity."

"Just a second, sir."

Click-buzz.

George's mind whirred. What could he say?

"Maternity. Dr. Johnson."

"Yeah—um—" George very carefully lowered his voice and slowed his words to a casual pace. "Hello. I'm staying at the Sea Shadows Inn just outside Mendocino? Well, I was in my room and I heard this groaning sound from next door. Well, I knocked on the door and

I found this—this lady—who I'd never seen before in my entire life—in labor, and—"

"Let's start with your name, sir."

"*My*—uh, look, do you really have to know that?"

"Uh-huh."

"Well, I really don't understand why, but it's George Peterson."

"Swell, Mr. Peterson. Now, how far apart are her labor pains coming?"

"Well, I didn't time it exactly, but I'd guess about three—two minutes apart."

"What's her name and who's her doctor?"

"Hold on." He cupped the receiver and yelled, "Doris what's your name and who's your doctor?"

"Joseph Harrington. Pine Street in Oakland."

"Joseph Harrington. Pine Street in Oakland," George repeated, "and her doctor's name is Doris."

"All right. We'll call him. Can you get a car and get her over here fast?"

"Yeah. Of course. I mean, it's certainly the least I can do for a perfect stranger. Doctor—uh—could you answer a question? I was just—uh—would—uh—erotic contact during the last stages of pregnancy be the cause of premature—"

"What? Of course not. Why would—"

"No reason. I just wondered."

"Well do the rest of your wondering in the car. We'll have her doctor meet her here. What's her last name?"

"Peterson."

"Peterson?"

"Baker."

"Right. Goodbye, Mr. Smith."

George hung up. "They're phoning your doctor. He'll meet us at the—Doris?"

She was standing in the doorway, pale. George turned paler. "Doris, what's the matter?"

"I don't think we'll make it to the hospital, George. My water just broke."

He bent over double as a terrible labor pain shot

through his stomach. The pain was even worse than when Debbie was born.

"Honey," she was saying. "I think we better find a doctor in the area."

George bolted upright. "But what if we *can't?*"

"Oh, George. You look terrible. You're not gonna faint?"

"Doris," he erupted, "I'm not a cab driver! I don't know how to deliver babies!"

"Oh my God, George. This is no time to start acting like Butterfly McQueen. Just get the nearest doctor on the phone." She collapsed to the bed.

He ran to the phone.

"Mr. Chalmers? It's George again. Look, can you get the nearest doctor on the phone? Fast! It's an emergency."

Doris made another terrible *Oooooooooooooh.*

He sat on the bed, grabbing her hand. "It's okay—it's okay. Hold on, just—hold on. Can you hold on? You okay?"

She stopped moaning and smiled weakly. "That'll teach you to fool around with a married woman."

"Sssh!" he said, panicked, as someone on the phone said, "three-seven-one."

"What?"

"Doctor Wilson's Service."

"Service?"

"Answering service."

"*Answering* service? What the hell kind of answer is that? You don't understand! She's in the last stage of labor!"

"Listen, buddy. Don't yell at *me*, I just deliver messages. The doctor's on his boat."

"On his boat?" George winced again as Doris moaned. "Then get me another doctor," he snapped.

"What do you mean?"

"You're a goddam *answering* service, aren't you? You know who the doctors are and where they are now. Find one who's around and get him to the—"

"*Oooooooooooooooh.*"

"*Doris, what is it?*"

"*I can—feel the baby!*"

"*Sea Shadows Inn,*" he screeched at the phone, and hung it up. "*No!*" he barked at Doris. He rose from the bed and started backing away. He was going to faint. He was no-kidding goddamn going to faint.

"*George, do something!*"

He grabbed the piano bench for support. "Lie back . . . relax," he said, woozy.

"*George, do something!*"

He sat on the bench. For a moment he stared at her. Doris was scared. She was sweating and pale and crying and scared and she needed him.

He ran to the bathroom.

"George—don't *leave* me!"

"I'm here. I'm right here," he said with command. "Hold on, baby." He reached for some towels. He was going to be fine. She was going to be fine. He raced to the bedroom. "It's okay. I'm here." He started to spread the towels on the bed.

"What . . . what are those for?" she said in a small tear-choked voice.

"Honey," he announced, "we're gonna have a baby."

"We?"

"Right," he said, "but I'll need your help. Come on. Give me your hand." He took it, and held it, tightly, in his own. "Look at me, honey. You're going to be fine. Just fine. There's nothing to worry about. We're together. You think I play the piano well?—Wait'll you see how I deliver babies. Okay, baby. Ready when you are. . . ."

STOP THE BOMBING

RALLY-NOON FEB. 26, 1965
At the Lincoln Mall

COME!

(1) Return books
(2) Bake banana bread for Harry's Mother
(3)
(4) Go.

TEN

"So tell me," Doris said, zipping up her jeans and picking up the Indian beaded headband, "I want to know—Oh—Gee, this is pretty. Thank you, Liz." Doris put it on.

"Well," Liz said, "it's an acquired taste that you seemed to have acquired. It's Yuni, by the way. And I don't want to tell you the American Indians have gone commercial, but when I saw this little fellow I bought the thing from, he was sitting on his blanket in the middle of the desert holding up a sign that said, YUNI-SEX JEWELS."

"You just made that up."

"I just made that up. Lately I've felt a compulsion to prove I can make things up without smoking peyote, you know what I mean? Those dope fiends are getting to be terrible snobs."

"Mmm. Well, we'll rap about dope fiends later. Now, I want to hear how Mexico went."

"Strange," Liz said, and picked some imaginary lint from the bed and then quickly brushed it from her black linen suit. "Or as somebody said: A mexican divorce is like a Mexican hat-dance. Very clumsy, but *very* fast." She paused to light a Virginia Slim, and looked around for something to do with the match. "You got an ashtray?"

"I quit smoking. But there's one in the kitchen. Along with some wine. We could use a little wine."

"And then again, some of us could use a little Scotch."

"Now—" Doris said, as they settled in the living

room, glasses in hand, "Mexican hat-dance—tell me all about it."

"Well," Liz shrugged, "there's nothing to tell. First, they take you to City Hall to, quote, 'establish residence,' which means you sign a book. Then they take you to a little stucco room with twenty other people waiting around and somebody calls out something that sounds like, 'Feenk! Feenk!' and after a while a startled Mrs. Fink begins to interpret they're talking to her." Liz sipped her Scotch. "So then Mrs. Fink walks up to the desk and two minutes later she's walking away, looking totally bewildered and I watch this happen eight or nine times: Mrs. Fink would stop in the middle of the room, scratch her head and then shake it slowly and walk to the door. So I'm wondering what the hell's going on when somebody hollers, '*Hon*ace! *Hon*ace!' and I finally figure they're calling out 'Jones.' So I go to the desk, and this jacketless judge, who looks like something out of *Viva Zapata*, reads me off something entirely in Spanish, and I look at the guy who's supposed to be my lawyer, who's supposed to translate, and he looks at me and shrugs, 'I hno thpik a-heenglith,' and for this, he's getting three hundred bucks, so anyway—Zapata presents me with this silly paper to sign and I sign it and the goddamn thing is in Spanish and he looks at me and hollers, 'Gringo! Gringo!' and I'm getting upset, and then Mrs. Greengold came up to the desk. End of report. Except that I walked away from the desk, and then stopped dead in the middle of the room, scratched my head and then shook it slowly and walked out the door."

"And that was *it*?"

Liz nodded. "I still don't believe it. I called up Roger and I told him, 'We're divorced. Either that, or I just signed a Spanish contract for nine thousand acres of worthless land.' "

"How did he react?"

"Roger? Laughed. The problem is he still doesn't know why I left. As far as he's concerned, he's a social drinker. Anyway, that's that. I am free, blue, and thirty-nine, to paraphrase something, and how are you?"

Doris jumped up. "My banana bread's burning!"

"Does that sum it up?"

"No," Doris said, taking the loaf pan out of the oven. "Ha! It isn't burned. No. I'm okay. I'm terrific, in fact."

"And still seeing George?"

"Oh yeah. You know?—The thing that's so great about seeing George is every single year when we meet each other, we find that we've grown in the same ways."

"Mmm. Then I'd guess he's been growing a beard."

"Huh?" Doris stirred up the yogurt icing and tasted it.

"Well," Liz said, "the one thing *you've* been growing is hair."

Doris looked down at her waist-length hair. "I like it," she pronounced.

"Hey, so do I. You look younger now than you did when you were young. Besides, you can think of it as money in the bank—considering mine cost two hundred bucks."

"Really? Two hundred bucks for a fall?" Doris licked the spoon and wondered where yogurt had been all her life.

"Yeah. Well, the last one I had was a cheapie, and I wore it in the rain and the whole thing frizzed, so I thought, *I* know why this lady sold her hair. *She* couldn't do a thing with it, either."

"Well," Doris started frosting the bread, "I'm here to tell you we both look terrific," she smiled, "and terribly groovy and young. Oh wow!" She stuck a yellow candle on the bread, "You know I've know George since I *was* young. Wow, that's a mindblower. Fourteen years!"

"And you still never call each other in between?"

"Nope. That's to keep it in perspective, dig?"

"Nope. But I really envy you, Doris. Losing perspective is what I do best."

"Wrong." Doris looked at the kitchen clock, and

poured herself an encore of Bella Wine. "I think you've really got it together, you know? So you got into trouble, but you also got out. And you've got a great job and you'll be just fine." Doris frowned. "It's Sybil Burton I'm worried about."

"Sybil *Burton*?"

"Yeah! I mean—what the hell can you do when your husband leaves you for Elizabeth Taylor? You sure can't accuse him of rotten taste."

"Mmm. I hadn't considered her plight."

"You want to come with me to the bomb rally now?"

"Oh. No thanks." Liz grabbed her bag. "The way I feel, I think I'd rather get bombed. Well"—she stood—"have fun running barefoot through George's beard."

"Oh. You know?" Doris thought about that, "you know, I bet he really *does* have a beard?" She grinned.

"Hey, Doris?" Liz turned in the doorway.

"Yeah?"

"If you ever want to go to Mexico . . . there's a lawyer named Guardo who speaks English."

"I don't," Doris said, shaking her head. "*Adios, amiga.*"

"Yeah. . . . *Vaya con dios,*" Liz said.

ELEVEN

"Mr. Chalmers here?" Doris said to the woman who stood behind the desk; she was fiftyish, wearing a Pucci dress, with her ash-blond hair in a French twist.

"He's in back," she said, in a rather pleasantly froggy voice, "on a long-distance call. I'm Josephine Clark. Can I help you?"

"Yeah. Did Mr. Peters get here?"

"Mmm. Been here about twenty minutes. He was talking to Ang—to—Mr. Chalmers, but he's gone to his cottage. Would you like me to ring him?"

"Oh. No thanks—Could you just give me the key?"

The woman gave her a curious look. "Are you—uh—traveling with him?"

"Uh-huh." Doris put her duffel bag down, as the woman turned to the rack with the keys. She put on some glasses and studied the rack.

"Sorry," she said, "I just came here last week, but you'd think I'd be able to find a 'seven.' Here it is. Right between six and eight." She turned and handed the keys to Doris along with another peculiar look.

Doris stopped at the Powder Room now. She studied herself in its oval mirror. She was wearing a nifty tie-dyed shirt, jeans, and a headband. She looked terrific. She looked twenty-eight. If the woman wanted to look at her strangely, that was clearly the woman's problem. Doris slung her duffel bag over her shoulder and, whistling, walked through the rest of the lobby and out to the garden. The day was warm. The sun was shining. Doris felt sexy. She ran to the cottage and breezed through the door.

"Hey man," she hollered. "Whaddaya say?"

George turned around. She ran to his arms, bear-hugged him, kissed him, and let out long groan of content. "So—wanna fuck?"

He froze, frowned. "*What?*" he said.

She grinned. "You didn't understand the question?"

"Of course I did." He was scowling now. "I just think it's a damned peculiar way to begin a conversation."

"Oh," she said.

Nodding slowly, she backed to the bed, and curled herself up on it, chewing a nail. George continued unpacking his bag. She looked him over. He did not have a beard; not only that—the rest of his hair looked like it was trying to join the Marines. He was wearing a dark, vested suit, the kind of suit it was nice to visit—in the Smithsonian—but certainly no place you'd like to live. But what got to her most was the set of his mouth. It was perfectly skinny with . . . disapproval?

"I was just—uh—trying to break the ice," she said cheerfully. "Thought you might be horny after your flight."

"Well, I didn't fly," he said. "I drove."

"From Connecticut?"

"Of *course* I didn't drive from Connecticut."

"Well . . . some people do."

"Well, I don't. I drove from L.A. We moved to Beverly Hills."

She whistled. "Far out," she said.

"No. It's rather close to Santa Monica, in fact."

"Oh . . ." she said slowly. "How come you moved?"

"A number of reasons." He finished unpacking and looked at her now. "For one thing"—he walked to the closet and put away his bag "—I got fed up with standing knee-deep in snow trying to scrape the ice off my windshield with a credit card." He turned. "Besides—there's a lot of people out there with a lot of money who don't know what to do with it."

"And you tell them?"

He was lighting a cigarette. "I'm what they call a Business Manager."

"Oh. . . . Things going okay?"

"I can't complain. Why?"

"You look kinda shitty."

He showed her his Disappearing Mouth act again.

"George, are you all right?"

"I'm fine." He stubbed his cigarette and poured himself a drink.

"You sure—something isn't bothering you?"

"Yes. You." He looked at her. "When did you join an Indian tribe? You look like a refugee from the Sunset Strip."

"From Berkeley," she said evenly. "I went back to school."

"To school? Why?"

She grinned. "You mean, what do I want to be when I grow up?"

"Well you have to admit," he said a little more softly, "it's a bit odd becoming a schoolgirl at your age."

"Are you kidding? Listen, it's not easy being the only one in the class with a clear skin."

He was pacing around. Watching him smoke made her desperately want a sunflower seed. She got up and fumbled around in her bag.

"What made you do it?" He sat on the bed.

"Want some?" She offered the packet of seeds. He squinted at her. She shrugged, and sat in the lotus position on the floor, eating. "Well . . . it was a dinner party that finally pushed me into it. Harry's boss invited us to dinner and I just freaked."

"Freaked," he said dryly.

"Flipped out?"

"Went crazy?"

"Got scared," she explained.

"Oh. Go on."

"Well, anyway, I'd spent so much time with the kids I didn't know if I was capable of carrying on an intelligent conversation with anyone over the age of five. Okay, so I went, and at dinner I was seated next to the boss. Well, I really surprised myself. He talked—then I talked—you know, just like a real conversation. Everything was cool until I noticed him looking at me wierdly as though I'd freaked out."

"Got scared?"

"Went crazy."

"Oh. Go on."

"Well, at this point, I looked down at his plate and realized that all the time we'd been talking, I'd been—cutting up his *meat* for him? Well, that's when I decided to get out of the house."

He kicked off his shoes. "But why school?"

"Why not? I don't know . . ." She pulled herself up and walked to the window. "It's hard to explain. I felt restless and—I don't know—undirected, and I thought an education might give me some answers."

"What kind of answers?"

She shrugged. "I don't know. Like, to find out where it's really at."

"Jesus."

"What's the matter?" She turned.

"That goddamned expression."

"Okay," she said. "Then how about 'to find out who the hell I am' ?"

"You don't get that kind of answer from a classroom."

"Well . . . I'm not in a classroom all the time. Boy, I tell you. The demonstrations are a learning experience in themselves."

"Demonstrations of what?"

She was losing patience. "Not 'of,' George. Against."

"Okay. *Against* what?"

"The *war*, of course. My God, Didn't you hear about it, George? It was in all the papers."

"Demonstrations," he snapped, "are sure as hell not gonna stop the war."

"You got a better idea?"

"Look, I didn't come here to discuss politics."

"Great! So far you've turned down sex and politics. You want to try religion?"

"I think I'll try a Librium."

"I think I'll take a walk."

Christ!

He took a pill.

It was amazing!

To think that Doris—*his* Doris—had turned out to be a freaky, hippie weirdo.

He lay on the bed and stared at the ceiling.

He felt angry, and vaguely sad.

It was as though this stranger had kidnapped Doris—or like *Invasion of the Body Snatchers*—just taken her over and swallowed her up.

It was awful.

But that was life.

It was one damned bad break after another.

And yet . . .

Man!

She kicked a stone.

What a bummer!

To think that George—*her* George—had turned out to be a stiff-lipped, uptight downer. She sat on a bench and stared at the pond.

She felt angry and terribly zapped.

It was as though this stranger had murdered George—as though he were dead, and she'd never get to see him—hold him again.

It was awful.

But that was life.

Its nature was change, said the *I Ching*.

But still . . .

He was walking down the path as she was walking up it.

"Come on, let's have dinner," he said.

"Okay."

"Double Scotch," George said.

"White wine," said Doris.

The waiter nodded, and walked away.

Doris looked around. The dining room had been done over this year. There were lots of plants. She was good with plants. She remembered he'd once said he had a brown thumb. She felt tender toward his thumb, and reached for his hand.

Angus and Miss What's-her-face entered the dining room. Clark. Josephine Clark. A nice neutral subject.

"How's Angus?" she began.

George smiled. "He's fine. Good old Angus."

"Who's Miss Clark?"

He shrugged. "She's kind of nice. He told me he needed an assistant manager. Says he's too old to run the place alone."

Doris looked at them. Angus and the woman were sitting at a table, the table, in fact, where Doris once sat demolishing a porterhouse steak from a stranger. "Mmm," she mused. "I bet they fall in love."

"Oh Christ. The Love Generation is speaking."

"*George,*" she said. "Why are you so uptight?"

"Oh Christ. That's another expression I hate."

"Uptight?"

"There's no such word," he announced.

"You know, you remind me of the time I was nine and I asked my mother what"—

The waiter came back, bringing the drinks. He left.

—"what *fuck* meant. You know what she said? 'There's no such word.' "

"Swell. And now that you've found out there is, you feel compelled to use it in every other sentence?"

"George, what's *bugging* you?"

"Bugging me. Right. I'll tell you what's 'bugging' me. The blacks are burning down the cities, there's a Harvard professor telling my kids the only way to happiness is to become doped-up zombies, and I have a teen-age son with hair so long that from the back he looks exactly like Yvonne De Carlo. That's what's 'bugging' me."

"Ooo." She watched him gravely. "That's a sign of age, honey."

"What is?"

"Being worried about The Declining Morality Of The Young. Besides," she shrugged, "there's nothing you can do about it."

"We could *start* by setting some good examples."

She cocked her head at him. Hopeless. Not a shred of

irony there. He wasn't kidding. She was starting to really get worried about him.

"My God," he continued, sipping his drink, "when I was checking in at the desk before, there was a bunch of hippies standing out front—boys and girls—and I said to Angus, 'are they coming in *here*?' and he told me they were only asking directions and I said, 'well, I hope you told 'em where to go!' " He was shaking his head. "I mean, Doris—they were probably seventeen and they're already—*living*."

"By that, I gather you mean 'In Sin.' "

"Yes, In sin! I mean they're carrying on like the bunch of wild Indians they look like."

"Mmm." She nodded. That explained the curious look at the desk. Miss Clark, undoubtedly trying to figure what Pocahontas was doing with The Right Reverend Peters. Poor darling. Poor George. She smiled cajolingly and squeezed his hand. "Well, when you were younger," she checked his eyes, "you weren't exactly a monk yourself. And look how splendidly *you* turned out."

"That," he announced tersely, "was different. Our relationship wasn't based on a casual one-night stand."

"Right. It's been *fifteen* one-night stands."

"It's still not the same. We've *shared* things. My God, I helped deliver your child. Remember?"

"Remember?" she stroked his hand. "I think of that as our finest hour."

For a moment, he smiled at her slowly, tenderly; for a moment, it looked like *George* had come back.

The waiter came back, shoving a wall of menus between them.

George immediately studied the menu. Shrugging, Doris looked at it too.

"Broiled sole," George decided. "And a tossed salad."

"Cannelloni," Doris said. "And some garlic bread?"

The waiter left. Chalmers came over to the table for a while. He wasn't, she noticed, wearing a tie and his silver-white hair was pleasantly shaggy.

George gave him Valuable Tips on The Market.

The food came.

Doris decided she wasn't too hungry.

"So"—George said—"How *is* the baby?"

"For one thing, not such a baby any more. She just had her fourth birthday."

"Mmm. Time flies."

In charity, Doris ignored that statement. "Aside from that, she's very healthy, very noisy, and very spoiled."

He speared a tomato. "And you don't feel guilty about leaving her alone while you go to school?"

"She's not alone. Harry's home a lot. The insurance business hasn't been too good lately."

"And how does he feel about it? I mean, your running away to school?"

"When I told him I wanted to go back to school because I wanted some identity, he said, 'You want identity? Go build a bridge. Invent penicillin, but get off my back.' "

George was smiling. "Always thought Harry had a head on his shoulders."

She put down her fork. "George, that was the *bad* story about him."

He didn't answer, just finished his fish.

"How's Helen?" she said.

He looked up sharply. "Helen's fine. She's just fine. . . . You want some Sanka?"

"No. I'm fine. I'd just as soon go."

He paid the check. They walked to the lobby and out to the grounds. The only sound in the balmy air was the chirring of crickets. She smelled eucalyptus, a trace of hibiscus. "Tell me," she said as they entered the cottage, "tell me a story that shows how really rotten Helen can be."

He looked at her. "That isn't like you," he said.

Shrugging slightly, she flopped to the bed. "Well, we seem to need something to bring us closer. I thought maybe a really lousy story about Helen would make you—you know, appreciate me more."

At least he smiled. "Okay." He sat on the edge of the

bed. "Well . . . as you know, she has this funny sense of humor."

"By funny, I take it you mean peculiar."

"Right. And it comes out at the most inappropriate times. I had signed this client—very proper, old money." He *straightened his tie?* "Well," he went on, "Helen and I were invited to his house for cocktails to get acquainted with him and his wife. Well, it was all pretty awkward to begin with, but we managed to get through the drinks all right. Then, as we went to leave, instead of walking out the front door, I walked into the hall closet."

Doris bit a smile.

"Now that wasn't so bad," he continued. "I mean, *any*body can do that. The mistake I made was I *stayed* in there."

"You *stayed* in the *closet*?"

"Well . . . I wasn't sure if they'd seen me go in. I guess I figured I'd stay there awhile till they'd all gone away. Okay, I admit it. I didn't think things through. I was in there for about a minute before I realized I'd well, misjudged the situation. When I came out, the three of them were just staring at me. All right, it was an embarrassing situation, but I probably could have carried it off. Except for what Helen did. You know what she did?"

Doris shook her head.

"She peed on the carpet."

"What?"

"You heard me, she peed on the carpet. Oh, not right away. First, she laughed. Her face was all screwed up and she held her sides and tears started rolling in streams down her face. Then she peed on their Persian rug."

Doris couldn't help it. The laughter erupted out of her mouth. Her face was screwed up, and she held her sides. She clamped a hand on her errant lips and managed to choke out, "What did you say?"

He looked at her coolly. "I *said,* 'You'll have to excuse my wife. Ever since she had that kidney transplant, she's had a problem.' Then I offered to have the rug cleaned."

Except for a couple of stray giggles that were trapped in her stomach, Doris was practically back in control. "Did that help?"

He shrugged. "They said it wasn't necessary. They had a maid."

She nodded somberly, and then those pressurized giggles came out. They came out in gasps and terrible whoops.

"You think this is *funny*?"

She nodded, laughing. "Oh George, I've been meaning to tell you for years—I just love Helen." She continued to laugh.

"Swell," he snapped. "Would she come off any worse if I told you I lost the account?" He glared.

It sobered her. Slowly, she shook her head. "George? When did you get so . . . *stuffy*?"

"*Stuffy?*" He was up and pacing again. "Am I 'stuffy' because I don't like my wife to urinate on my clients' rugs?"

"I didn't mean just that, but—well—"

"Well, what?"

"Well, *look* at you! I mean, you scream—Establishment!"

He folded his arms. "I am not a faddist, if that's what you mean."

"What do you mean?"

He poured himself a drink. "I have no desire to be like those middle-aged idiots with bell-bottomed trousers and Prince Valiant haircuts who go around saying '*ciao,*' is what I mean."

"Honey, I wasn't talking about *fashion*. I was talking about—your attitudes."

"My attitudes are what they always were. I haven't changed at all."

"Oh yes, you have. You used to be crazy and—and insecure and a terrible liar and—*human*. Now you seem so—*sure* of yourself."

He laughed bitterly. "That's the last thing I am."

"Oh?" That stopped her. She cocked her head and leaned back on the pillows.

He drank and paced. "I picked up one of Helen's magazines the other day. And there was this article—telling women what kind of *orgasms* they should have. It was called 'The Big O. . . .' " He sat on the edge of the bed. "You know what really got to me? This was a magazine my mother used to buy for its *fruitcake recipes.*"

She smiled at him, fondly. "The times, they are a-changing, darling."

"Yeah." He rubbed his eyes. "Too fast . . . too fast." Shaking his head, he took off his jacket and loosened his tie. "I don't know," he mused. "Twenty-thirty years ago we had standards—all right—maybe they were black and white, but at least—at least they were standards. I don't know. Today"—he shook his head again—"it's so . . . confusing."

"Well at least that's a step in the right direction." She kissed him, tenderly. It felt very good to have him in her arms. When he moved away, he was frowning slightly, in a soft kind of way.

"When did I suddenly become so appealing?"

"When you went from pompous to confused." She grinned. "So what's your pleasure? A good book, a walk by the ocean, or me?"

"You."

"Thought you'd never ask." She whipped her shirt off over her head. When she looked at him again, he was frowning again; not so softly. "What's the matter *now*?"

"Doris! You're not—wearing a bra!"

She giggled. "Oh, George. You're so—forties!" She put her arms around him and nibbled his ear.

"I happen," he said, "to be an old-fashioned man."

"Mmm." She was moving her lips toward his mouth. "Next thing you'll tell me you voted for Goldwater."

"I did."

She suddenly pulled away. "You're putting me on."

"No."

He wasn't. She could tell by his eyes. She grabbed her shirt and stalked from the bed.

"What're you—what're you *doing*?" he sputtered.

She wheeled. "If you think I'm going to bed with any goddamn son of a bitch who voted for Goldwater, man, you're nuts."

"Doris," he yelped, "you can't *do* this to me. Not *now!*"

"Oh can't I!" She put on her shirt. "I'll tell you something. Not only will I not go to bed with you now, I will not go to bed with you retroactively! I want back fifteen years of fucks."

"Doris! Don't be ridiculous!"

"How could you *vote* for a man like that?"

"Could we discuss this later?"

"No!" she barked. "We'll discuss it now—why?"

"Because I've got a son who wants to be a rock musician. Now will you please come back to—"

"What the hell kind of reason is that?"

"The best one I can come up with in my present condition. Doris, will you please—"

"Sorry, you'll have to do better than that." She folded her arms. "I want a reason."

"Okay!" He zipped up his fly and stood. "Okay, he was going to end the war."

"By destroying the country."

"He never said that. That's the trouble with you people. You never listen."

"You . . . *people?*" She held up a hand. "Forget about that, forget about that. I will not let this sink to a personal level. The point is, George, it's a civil war. We have no right being there at all in the first place."

"Oh Christ," he fumed. "I'm sick of hearing that liberal crap. We've got the bomb. Why don't we use it?"

"Are you *serious*?" She gave him a squinting glare.

He looked at her levelly, nodding slowly. "Yes. I'm serious." His voice was bitter. "Wipe the sons of bitches off the face of the earth." He walked to the piano and poured himself a drink.

Doris couldn't move. Her mouth was open and she

couldn't close it. After a while, it moved by itself. "My God," it said. "My God," she added. "I don't—I don't know anything about you. What—what kind of a man *are* you?"

"Right now?" he said acidly. "Very frustrated."

"All this time"—she sank, bewildered, to the arm of the couch—"I thought I was going to bed with a liberal democrat . . ." She looked up sharply. "You told me you worked for *Stevenson,*" she accused.

He sighed, wearily. "That was a long time ago, Doris."

"What changed you? What happened?"

"I simply grew up."

"Yeah? Well you didn't turn out very well."

"Swell. Fine. Can we just forget it?"

"Forget it? How can I forget it? I mean being stuffy and—and old-fashioned is one thing, but being a Fascist is another."

"I am not a Fascist!"

"You're advocating mass murder!"

"Doris," he menaced, "drop it, okay. Just—drop it."

"I'd like to drop it right on your head. How could you *do* this to me? You stand for everything I'm against!"

"Then maybe you're against the wrong things!"

"You used to believe in the same things I do."

"I changed!"

"Why?"

"Because Michael was killed!"

They stared at each other.

She closed her eyes. "Oh dear God," she breathed softly. "H—how?"

He made a defeated shrug. When he spoke, his voice held a quiet calm. "He was trying to get a wounded man to a Red Cross copter and a sniper killed him." He moved to the window and looked through the panes at the dark garden.

"When?" she said softly.

"July second. We got the news at a July Fourth party. Helen went completely to pieces." He turned. "I didn't feel a thing. I thought I was in shock and it would hit me later." He looked at her slowly. "But you know something? It never did. The only emotion I've been able to feel is blind anger. I didn't shed a tear." He laughed ruefully and poured himself a drink. "Isn't that something? He was my son. I loved him. But for the life of me I can't . . . seem to cry over him. I"—he looked at her—"Doris, I'm sorry—about—everything. I've—lately I've just been a bit on edge and—" The glass he was holding slipped from his hand; he fumbled to save it but it smashed to the floor. "Terrific!" he barked. "Will you *look* at that?" He held up a bloody hand and stared at it. "Goddamn son of a bitch! If it's not one goddamn thing it's—"

And then he was suddenly sobbing, and she ran to him, holding him close in her arms, and he wept for a very long time.

Sea Shadows Inn

Feb. 11, 1972

Mr. George Peters
9379 Pointsetta Pl.
Los Angeles, Calif.

Dear Mr. Peters,

Just to confirm your reservation for Cottage 7, Feb. 25-27. Look forward to seeing you.

Best,

Angus

Angus Chalmers

monte verde, california

TWELVE

'Josie," Angus said, "who was that kid with the beard ust came in?"

Josephine looked up slowly from her needlepoint as ingus came ambling across the lobby. "You mean who vas just checking in before? That was no kid, that was Jeorge Peters."

"Mmph," Angus said, and laughed. "You may find his hard to believe, but to me, George Peters *is* a kid. Valter Cronkite's a kid. Henry Kissinger's a kid."

"Yes dear," she said, "and what does that make ne?"

"My child-bride."

"How pleasant." She smiled and put down the red-nd-green flamestitch pillow. "Angus . . . there's omething I have to confess."

"Yeah?"

"I lied about my age."

"I know."

"You know?"

He was tuning the television set. "Yep. You aren't ixty, you're sixty-three. Reason I know—look, the damn ox is pickin' up ghosts, I bet it's from the damn con-ominium they built, used to be able to look out from ere clear to the lake and not see a thing and now they ot a goddamn condominium, two McDonald's and a hopping center."

"Yes dear."

"You think I forgot what I was saying? I'm not that ld. Reason I know how you're sixty-three is account of ou're not a very logical liar. You can't just lie about your age, baby doll. You gotta fix all the other dates too."

"Oh?"

"You told me you were twenty when the stock market crashed."

"Angus, you have a terrible memory."

"I have a wonderful memory."

"That's what's terrible." Josephine laughed.

Angus got the ghosts to disappear from the set. Now there was a perfectly sharp, clear image of a purple housewife with an orange hairdo holding up a jar of bright green cheese. "Anyway," he said, "you're still just a kid. The year you were twenty, I was fightin' off the Rocco gang."

"Rocco gang?"

"Buncha bootleggers. Decided they wanted control of this place. My father was gonna give in to 'em, too. Sell out and go." Angus laughed. "So me, the young Turk, I said, 'bananas to that,' came back from Frisco and kicked Rocco out."

"Angus—really?"

"Yeah. Really."

"You went up against a *gang*?"

The purple housewife was serving the green cheese to her kid, who was turning purple. Angus caught his own reflection in the screen: a tan, bony, white-haired man with a skinny neck. "You're married to one tough cookie, kid."

"How did you do it?"

"Played poker with him."

"What?"

"You heard me. Rocco thought he was king of the cards. Me, I was a dealer on Carmody's gambling boat on the bay. So I told him I'd play him Stud for the turf. If I won, he'd clear out. Well, first he just laughed at me, but Rocco was a sport so he said, 'Okay.' And I won. And that's that."

"And what would have happened if you'd lost?"

"Never mind. Point is, I won. Funny, you know"—Angus rubbed his jaw—"if it hadn't been for Rocco,

I'd've stayed on in Frisco . . . wouldn't've come back here and met Maggie, and God only knows what I'd be doin' today."

"Angus, you're fascinating. You never *told* me all that."

"Yeah. Well . . . I was saving those stories for when I get too old to do anything but talk."

"That'll be the day." Josie turned around as the door banged closed. Angus followed her glance: Doris was there, with a piece of that ugly brown plastic luggage with the little initials that everyone loved and that looked to Angus like brown plastic luggage with little initials, and as far as he could see, wasn't worth more than twelve bucks a throw. She was also wearing a big mink coat. He waved hello, as his wife got up and hurriedly crossed the lobby to greet her. Angus went back to watching the news.

A few minutes later Josie came back and sat down beside him on the newly recovered chintz-covered couch.

"If you want to know what you missed," Angus said, "the kid Cronkite said the kid Kissinger's holed up in Paris having secret peace talks, and McGovern's gonna speak in Frisco tomorrow."

"I wonder how it'll all turn out."

"The war or the election?"

"Doris and George."

"Doris and George? What do you mean?"

"Well"—she picked up her needlepoint again—"*he* comes in here with butterfly patches sewn on his jeans and a beard and a knapsack, and *she* comes in here like *Harper's Bazaar* and I just wonder . . . that's all I mean."

"Mmm," Angus said, and reached for her hand. "Well, if you want to worry about something, worry about me."

"About you?"

"Yeah. While you were gone"—he thumbed at the set—"I think I fell in love with Golda Meir."

THIRTEEN

George smiled, leaned back on the pillows, and blew a fat smoke-ring at the ceiling. The radio was playing "Gentle On My Mind." George felt gentle. He scratched his beard and let out a long, smoky yawn. Doris was lying there, smoking, beside him, her blond-streaked hair falling over one eye, and her bright red nails lightly drumming the bed. Saying nothing, he reached for her hand, stilling the drummers and earning a smile that made him feel warm all over again. Amazing, he thought. After twenty-one years they were still so goddamn hot for each other that the first kiss hello had carried them straight across the room to the bed. He closed his eyes, kneading her thigh, and then felt her moving, sitting up in bed.

He opened one eye and looked at her again. She'd put on her glasses and picked up a crossword puzzle and a pen. He lifted the slightly graying eyebrow that hovered over his open eye and sighed. If she needed words, he supposed, they should come from him, not the San Francisco paper.

"Hey?" he said.

"Mmm." She looked up.

"I was just thinking how great it still is after all these years."

"Honey," she put down the paper and smiled, "if you add up all the times we've actually made it, we're still on our honeymoon."

He laughed, rolling over to stub out his smoke.

"Hey, did I tell you I'm a grandma?" she said.

"Nope." He grinned. "But I think you picked a hell of a weird time to do it."

"Mmm." She pushed her glasses to the top of her head. "You think it's decadent having sex with a grandma?"

George thought it over. "Only with my own."

She laughed.

He stretched, and managed to knock the paper to the floor. "Anyway," he said, "you're the youngest-looking grandma I've ever had a peak experience with."

"Hah," she crowed, and got out of bed, putting on a brown satin kimono, and making a mock-Oriental bow. "My mother thanks you, my father thanks you, my hairdresser thanks you, and my plastic surgeon thanks you." Grinning, she backed to the dressing-table bench, sat, turned, and started doing her face, scanning it closely as she brushed on some rouge. She laughed again. "When Harry says, 'you're not the girl I married,' he really doesn't know how right he is."

"Didn't Harry like your old nose?"

She turned. "Harry thinks this *is* my old nose."

"He never noticed?"

She faced herself again with a tube of mascara. "Pathetic, isn't it? A new dress, I could understand. But a whole nose?"

George shrugged. "Well," he temporized, getting out of bed and reaching for his jeans, "well—to be totally honest, Doris, I really can't see much difference, either."

"Well, I don't care," she said breezily. "The point is, it's different from *my* end. Makes me *feel* more attractive, you know what I mean?"

"Mmm." He picked up his yellow T-shirt and pondered the alligator decal on the front. He mentally bobbed the alligator's nose. "And why" he said, pulling on the shirt, "do you feel you need validation of your attractiveness?" He watched her painting her mouth with a brush.

She shrugged. "Every woman gets a little insecure when she hits forty-four."

"Forty-five."

She nodded. "See what I mean? Anyway, that's this year's bad story about Harry. Got one about Helen?"

"Oh sure," he said cheerfully, reaching for his sandals. "Few months ago, there was this loud party next door. Well, Helen couldn't sleep and she didn't want to take a sleeping pill because she had to get up at six the next morning. So she took two pills and stuffed them in her ears. It worked. Only, during the night they melted! So the next morning as the doctor was digging this stuff from her ears, he said, 'You know—these *can* be taken orally.' " Laughing, he reached for his sunburst medallion. "Helen just laughed. I mean she doesn't care."

Doris was watching him. "If that's the worst story you can tell about your wife, you must be a very happy man."

"Well"—he shrugged—"let's say I've discovered the *potential* for happiness." He looked up quickly as the telephone rang, and then leaned in to grab it. Doris got there first.

"Hello?" she said tensely, and he watched as her shoulders seemed to sag just a little. "Oh . . . hi, Liz . . ." He walked to the piano and poured himself a glass of Evian water. Doris's shoulders were squared again. "No," she said into the phone, "it's *sixty,* not sixteen, *sixty* guests. . . . That's right. A brunch. We've catered a couple of parties for her before. No problem. She'll set up tables around the pool, and . . . yeah, that's right. . . ." George walked to the window. Obviously, Doris's business was doing well. What had started three years ago as a tea shop featuring home-baked banana bread with yogurt icing and special-order birthday cakes made with carrots had patently bloomed into something bigger. Obviously, *Doris* was doing well. On the other hand, just below the level of Obvious, George sensed she wasn't doing any too well. "Yes, Liz. Right. On the patio," she said, as George sipped his water and started to pace. "Oh, Liz?" He turned as her voice got tenser. "Just by any chance . . . did Harry call? . . . Oh." She turned now, facing the wall. "Oh.

well okay. I'll be at this number." She hung up the phone and turning, said, "Sorry, busy weekend. I had to leave this number."

He shrugged at that one. "Harry know you're here?"

"Oh no." She moved back to the makeup table. "Harry still thinks I go on retreat. Don't worry."

That rolled off his shoulders too. "I'm not." He studied her reflection in the mirror.

She looked up and caught him. "Then why are you frowning?"

"Because I'm getting bad vibes again."

She put down a hairbrush and tilted her head. "Again?"

He nodded. "When you first walked in, I picked up on your high tension-level. Then after we made love I sensed a certain anxiety reduction, but now I'm getting a definite negative feedback."

For an answer, she picked up the hairbrush again, and nodded. "When did you go into analysis?"

"How did you know I'd gone into analysis?"

"Oh," she said dryly, "just a wild guess." She rose abruptly and, hairbrush in hand, crossed to her suitcase and pulled out some wine-colored lounging pajamas. She examined them critically. "What made you start?"

"Well . . . let's say, my value system changed." He followed her in through the bathroom door, and sat on the edge of the tub as she dressed. "One day I just took a good look around at my hundred-and-fifty-thousand-dollar house, and the three cars, and the swimming pool, and the gardeners, and I thought—*Why?* I mean, did I want the whole status-trip thing. So—I decided to try and find out what I really did want, and who I was."

"Mmm," she turned her back and pointed at a zipper. He zipped it, and she went back to brushing her hair. "So you went from analysis to Esalen to Gestalt to Transactional to Encounter Groups to Nirvana."

He nodded, patient. "Honey, just because some people are trying to widen their emotional horizons doesn't make the experience any less valid." He lit a cigarette. "I've learned a lot."

"Mmm. I've noticed," she said flatly. "For one thing you learned to talk as though you're reasoning with someone about to jump off a high ledge."

He nodded, still patient. "I know," he said nicely. "I tend to overcompensate for my emotionalism and sometimes there's a certain loss of spontaneity. I'm working on that."

She smiled. Nicely. "I'm glad to hear it. What else have you learned?"

He thought about that, stroking his beard. "Well, I suppose the other thing I've learned is that . . . behind the walls I've built around myself I'm a warm, caring, loving human being."

She laughed. "I could have told you that twenty years ago." She kissed him on the cheek. "Free," she added and turning, walked to the living room again. Rising, he glanced in the bathroom mirror. He liked the beard. He liked the gray in it. He liked the fact that he could like to look at himself in the mirror. Honesty begins with looking in the mirror. If you can look yourself straight in the eye in the mirror, you're home free. George watched himself with honest eyes, made himself a peace sign and walked through the door.

Doris was on the sofa with a briefcase, going through papers. She looked up briefly. "So tell me—how's Helen reacting to your—uh—'voyage of self-discovery'?"

"Well," he sat at the piano and noodled, "at first she tended to overreact."

"Oh. In what way?"

"She threw a grapefruit at me in the A & P." He started to play "Satin Doll." "It was natural that we'd have some interpersonal conflicts to work through. But now it's cool. She's into pottery."

"And what are you into?"

"Hmm?" He'd found a really terrific chord. He played it again, wincing at its sweetness.

"Are you still in accounting?"

"Accounting? Of course not. Christ, I was never the accountant type."

"Sometimes you were, and sometimes you weren't.

How are you making a living, George?" She was watching him closely.

He stopped playing. "Well, we live very simply, Doris—we don't need much. And what we do need I can provide by simple, honest labor."

"Like what?"

"I play cocktail piano in a singles bar in the Valley."

The telephone rang. She jumped up to catch it. "Hello! . . . Oh . . . Yes, Liz . . . no way . . ." George started noodling chords again, softly. "Tell him that's our final offer. I don't care how good a location it is. . . . That's bull, Liz. He needs us more than we need him. Yeah. If he doesn't like it he can shove it, but don't worry—he won't. Anything else? . . . Okay, you know where to reach me. Bye." She hung up. "I'm buying another store."

"Oh?" He looked up slowly from an A-flat ninth diminished. "Why?"

"Money." She sat on the sofa again.

"Is that why you went into business? To make money?"

"No." She looked up quickly from her papers. "I also wanted some power too. And it finally penetrated my thick skull that attending C.R. groups with ten other frustrated housewives was not the way to get it."

"C.R. groups?" He started playing "Gentle On My Mind."

"Consciousness raising." Another quick look. "I take it you *are* for Women's Liberation?"

He grinned. "Hey, I'm for any kind of liberation."

She put down a contract. "That's a cop-out and you know it. Women have always been exploited by men."

He stopped playing and started to pace, yawning a little. "We've *all* been shafted, one way or another, Doris, and by the same things . . . Look," he turned, "let me lay this one on you. I go to a woman doctor. The first time she gave me a rectal examination, she said, 'Am I hurting you or are you just tense?' I said, 'I'm tense.' She said, 'Are you tense because I'm a woman?' and I said, 'No, I get tense when *anybody* does that to me. . . ." He sat down. "You see what I mean?"

She didn't seem to see. Or maybe she just wasn't *ready* to see. George had patience. She'd outgrow it. On the other hand, he personally thought militance was a semihostile overreaction not against the much-maligned Machismo, but that fact that men weren't macho *enough*. On the other hand, even though George considered that militance itself was a dishonest pose, Doris, it seemed was honestly militant, which made it okay. Until she outgrew it. She was signing a paper. She put it down.

"The only thing I know," she said with an honest tone of conviction, "is the only time a woman is taken seriously in this country is when she has the money to back up her mouth—And the business has given me that."

"Hey, listen," he said, watching her reaction, "I really think it's great that you've got a hobby."

"Hobby?!" she snapped, honestly indignant. "Last year we grossed over half a million dollars!"

"Cool," he said evenly. "Don't misunderstand me. I meant, by the way, that your hobby was money, and if that's what you want, then I'm very happy for you." He shrugged. "I'm just not into money any more."

She was staring at him strangely, with a look of amusement. "George," she said lightly, "Do you ever get the feeling we're drifting apart?"

"No. In some ways, I think we've never been closer."

"Really? I don't know, sometimes I think our lives are always—out of sync."

He was shaking his head. "We all realize our potential in different ways at different times. What I'm saying is, don't lay your trip on me. That's all."

"Then let me lay this on you." She reached into her briefcase and pulled out a check. "Here."

He gave her a quizzical look.

"It's the money you lent me to start the tearoom."

He glanced at it briefly. "It's three times what I gave you."

She shrugged. "Well of course. Return on your investment."

"Uh-huh." He sat on the sofa beside her, stretching his arms. "Sorry. I can't accept that, Doris."

"Oh yes you can."

He shook his head no.

"If you'd lent the money to a man, you'd take it."

He smiled slowly, his arms behind his neck. "If I don't take it, I'm a Male Chauvinist Pig, is that it?"

"And a dumb one." She smiled. "Besides, I don't like the idea of you having to play in a singles bar."

"On the other hand, I happen to dig it."

She nodded. "Yeah. That's the part I don't like."

"Jealous?"

"Don't be silly."

"I won't if you won't." He looked at the check and took it. "All right. I'll put it in the bank. I suppose my youngest, most liberated daughter will want to go to college or India or something, and in answer to your other question—no."

"What other question?"

"The one you didn't ask. No. I don't fool around in the bar. I just like the work there. I find it fulfilling. How about you? Does what you're doing give you a sense of fulfillment?"

"Fulfillment? Let me tell you about fulfillment."

She lit a cigarette. "The other day I went into Gucci's and I saw this suede suit that I liked and I asked this snooty salesman the price and he said, 'Seven hundred dollars' and started to walk away. So I said, 'I'll take five.' And he turned and said, 'Why on earth would you want five?' and I said, 'for my bowling team.' *That's* fulfillment."

George simply nodded. "In other words—you've got everything you want?"

"Mmm. With one minor exception. Somewhere along the way, I seem to have lost my husband." She laughed out a smoky *ha.*

"Lost him?"

"Well, I don't know if I've lost him or simply misplaced him. He walked out of the house four days ago and I haven't seen or heard of him since."

Nodding slowly, George studied her. "How do you feel about that? Honestly."

She took off her glasses and eyed him coolly. "George, do me a favor—stop talking as though you're leading a human potential group. It really pisses me off."

He grinned. "That's cool."

"*What's* cool?"

"For you to transfer your feelings of aggression and hostility from Harry to me." He nodded. "As long as you *know* that's what you're doing."

"You know something, George? You're really beginning to get on my nerves."

He grinned again. "That's cool, too."

"Jesus!" She got up quickly frow the couch and started to pace.

"I mean it," he said. "At least it's *honest*. Total honesty is the key to everything."

"Oh really?" She wheeled. "And are *you* being totally honest with Helen?"

"I'm trying, yes."

"Have you told her about us?"

"No, but I could." He frowned at her, fish-eye. "Really," he said, "I think that today she's mature enough to handle—"

"George, you're full of shit!"

He considered that honestly. "I can buy that," he decided, and thought again, "if you're being totally honest."

"*Believe* me, I'm being totally honest!"

"Swell," he said. "At least it's a start. But what about that other garbage? 'I don't know if I lost him or simply misplaced him.' I mean, what sort of crap is that?"

For a moment she looked at him; then she put her glasses down on the table. "Okay," she said quietly, and sat. "You've got a point."

"My point is, how do you feel about this?"

"Dammit, George. You're *doing* it again."

He said nothing.

"All right," she conceded. "I think—"

"Nope! Don't tell me what you think. Tell me how you feel."

"Like I've been kicked in the stomach."

"What else?"

"Angry! Hurt. Betrayed. And—okay, a little guilty. But you know something? I *resent* the fact that he's making me feel guilty."

"Why do you feel resentment?" he pressed.

"Listen," she flared, "I didn't marry Harry because he had a good head for business. Okay, it so happens I discovered I did. Or maybe I was just lucky—I don't know. The point is, I don't love Harry any less because he's a failure as a provider. Why should he love *me* any less because I'm a success? . . . I don't know . . ." shrugging, she shook her head. "One of these days I'm going to know exactly how I *do* feel."

"You don't know?"

"It varies between Joan of Arc, Rosalind Russell, and Betty Crocker."

"Well," he mused, "I suppose women are going through a transitional period."

"Yeah, but what'll we do till it's over?"

"Have you tried telling him you still love him?"

"Love him? Why the hell else does he think I've been hanging around for twenty-seven years?"

"Yeah, except now you've got to deal with now. I mean, just right now his masculinity is being threatened and probably needs some reassurance, you know—some validation of his worth as a man."

"And how the hell am I supposed to do that? I mean, that's some trick."

George shook his head. "No. Just total honesty, honey. Is it so hard for you to tell him you understand how he feels?"

"Right now it is; yes."

"Oh?"

She bolted up again and paced again. He vaguely remembered when he himself had been that tense and cut off from his feelings. Till four months ago. It seemed another world.

"I mean why the hell should I have to apologize," she bristled, "for doing something *well*? I mean, it's *his* damn ego that's messing us up. I really *resent* that."

"You want him back?"

There was a much longer pause than George had expected. Finally she said, "I'm not sure I do." She paused. "Ask me tomorrow and I'll probably give you a different answer."

Frowning, he cocked his head at her. "Why?"

"Because," she said, "tomorrow I won't have you."

He looked at her. "I'm always with you in spirit."

She laughed a little harshly. "Yeah, well it's not easy to put your cold feet on somebody's spirit. Especially when they're four hundred miles away." She turned, rather quickly, away from his eyes and looked out the window.

"Was that a proposal?" he asked softly.

She turned again. "You interested?"

"Are you?"

"I—I've always thought we'd make a nice couple."

"You didn't answer the question."

"No, *you* didn't answer it—I was the one who proposed." She laughed again. "Don't look so panicky, George. I'm only three-quarters serious."

"Well . . . when you're completely serious, ask me again."

"I bet you say that to all the girls."

He shook his head, watching her.

"Thanks," she said gently.

"And stop feeling so insecure," he added.

"Me?"

He nodded. "You're as feminine now as you always were."

She was silent for a moment; then she smiled. "I know Gloria Steinem would hate me, but oh *boy*, am I glad you said that." She smiled again, a soft-warm, Last-Year's-Doris smile and moved to his arms. He held her, his soft-warm, all-time Doris, and kissed her; she rested her head on his chest. "I guess I'm not as emancipated as I thought I was, huh?"

"None of us are."

"I'm sorry," she said. "Oh George, I'm sorry for being so—well, so bitchy before."

"You weren't being bitchy. You were just—"

"Don't say it."

"What?"

"Dishonest."

He grinned at her. "*I* didn't say it," he said.

"Mmm." She was running her hand through his beard. "I love you," she said a little bit sadly, and before he could answer she said, "You hungry?"

He nodded.

"Well, you're in luck," she grinned, "because tonight our dinner is being catered by the chicest, most expensive French delicatessen in San Francisco."

"How'd we swing that?"

"The owner," she said, stroking his beard, "has a Thing about you." She moved to the door. "It's in the trunk of my car."

"The owner's Thing?"

She giggled.

"You need any help?" he said.

"Yes. Set the table, light the candles, and when I come back, make me laugh."

"I'll try."

"That's okay. If you can't make me laugh, just hold my hand." She stood in the doorway and watched him for a moment, very tenderly, before she left.

Staring at the door, he lit a cigarette and absently started clearing the table, wondering, honestly, what he would have done if she'd really been serious.

Would he really have left Helen?

Reaching for the picnic basket in the trunk, she wondered how serious she'd honestly been.

Had she spoken before out of Injured Pride?

Or did she really want to marry George?

Or had the idea really panicked him?

Which?

Or did she really want Harry back?

Or was it both?

George looked up at the ringing phone. He hesitated. It was Tony Bella or Helen . . . or Liz. Who probably Knew. He picked up the phone:

"Hello?"

"Is—uh—Doris Baker there?" said a guy who sounded like Broderick Crawford.

"No," George said, sounding a little like Henry Aldrich, clearing his throat and also his mind of the notion the caller could really be Harry. "Who's calling?"

"Harry. Her husband."

"Uh-huh. Well Harry, this is the wrong—" it was too late to say it was the wrong number, he'd already asked, 'who's calling?'—"time to reach her, she just—uh—hold on—hold on for a minute."

He looked out the window. Doris was opening the trunk of the car; she was also talking to Josephine Chalmers. George looked back at the waiting phone. George did several hours of thinking in twenty seconds. He picked up the phone.

"Hello," he said in a voice that sounded like the voice of a man you could leave your wife with for twenty-one weekends and feel you were leaving her in honorable hands, "Listen," he continued in this deep, reliable, competent voice, "listen, Harry, we're two adult, mature human beings and I've decided to be totally honest with you. Doris will be back in a couple of minutes but meanwhile, I'd like to talk to you myself—because—because I know you and Doris have been having some problems and you see, she and I have been very close friends, what I mean is, I've known her for twenty-one years and through her, I feel as though I know you. Well, let me make that a little bit clearer. When I say I've known her for twenty-one years, I mean I've only known her on one weekend, I mean we've been meeting this same weekend for twenty-one years. You see, Harry, when she goes on retreat—well, we can get into that part later, but first I want you to know something. She loves you, Harry. I know she does. Listen, maybe if I told you a story she told me about you, you might understand. Are you listening? Listen—a while ago, Doris was supposed to act as a den mother for your ten-year-old daughter and her Indian Guide group. Well, she got hung up at the store and was two hours late, and by the time she got home and looked in the living room, you know what she saw? A rather overweight, balding, middle-aged man with a feather on his head sitting cross-legged on the floor, very gravely and gently telling a circle of totally absorbed little girls what it was like to be in a World War Two Japanese prison camp. She turned around, walked out, and sat in her car, and thanked God for being married to a man like you. You understand me, Harry? And if she hasn't been telling you how much she loves you, it's just because sometimes married people get into a kind of emotional straightjacket and find it difficult to express how they truly feel about each other. What I mean is, total honesty, Harry, total honesty is always the key. And while we're on the subject of honesty, Harry, I want to tell you that, yes, I've known Doris for twenty-one years and I'm not a bit ashamed to admit that it's probably been the most intimate . . . satisfying . . . rewarding experience I've had in my life."

"Hey, who the hell is this?"

"My name?" George stared at the Moment Of Truth—"My name?"—the moment of Total Honesty—"My name is Father Michael O'Herlihy."

Sea Shadows Inn

Feb. 1, 1977

Dear Friends:

Due to the rising costs of labor and electricity, we've been forced once again to increase our rates. A new rate-card is enclosed.

We hope this causes you no inconvenience.

Sincerely,

Lawrence Chalmers

Lawrence Chalmers
Manager

monte verde, california

FOURTEEN

"Well, I had to do *something*." Liz did a sit-up by the edge of the pool. Sitting, she rapidly jutted her chin, sticking her tongue out and straining her neck in what she'd explained was a yoga position and "why you never see a Tibetan monk with a double chin." She got to her feet and then, bending over, instantly touched them. Doris sighed. Liz, in a Danskin, was too much to have to face in the morning. Or too little. Liz was a trim, taunt, size 8. On the other hand, Doris quickly reasoned, she'd never had children. On the other hand, Doris quickly remembered, Doris herself had never come close to being an 8, even *before* she'd had any children. Doris tried holding her stomach in now. By the time she got it in, Liz had touched her toes a half-dozen times.

"It was a question," Liz said, "of cushioning the jolt of being fifty. For a while I considered adopting a child." She straightened, and stretched her arms to the sky. "But I decided instead to take one for a lover."

"What?"

"He's thirty."

"I see what you mean."

"He's wonderful, Doris. He's a solar engineer."

"What the hell's that?" Doris stretched on the chaise.

"Solar energy?"

"Oh."

"He puts gizmos on people's roofs. I'm thinking of letting him put one on mine."

"Nice," Doris said. "When it's over you won't be losing a lover, but gaining a sun."

Liz just laughed and started running in place. "It's dawned on me," she said, not a whit out of breath, "that the measure of a relationship is not how long it lasts, but how happy it makes you. Live for today." She stopped running and seemed to throw herself down at the ground, catch herself, and do a push-up. "The *attitudes* today are so much—*uch*—better. When I think of the Mickey Mouse crap we went through—*uch*." She stopped pushing and rolled to her back.

"Even so," Doris said, sipping a Tab, "if everything's really so wonderful now, how come they dress up like nineteen-thirty and run to old movies? Romance is missing, isn't it?"

"Well . . . you can't have everything."

"Mmm," Doris mused. "Not all at once. But it seems to me—if you live long enough—you get a bit of everything piece by piece. Rich, poor, sickness, health, better, worse, sex, romance—"

"And old," Liz added. "Boy, I tell you. I'm starting to look at little old ladies and wonder which one I'm gonna turn out to be. The scrawny one or the fat one. The one who talks to herself in the street or the one who talks to everyone else."

"You've still got a while to go," Doris said.

"But whiles seem to go a lot faster these days."

"True . . ." Doris nodded and looked toward the house, where Harry was sitting on a patio chaise, playing This Little Piggie with Tony's "new" baby, who was already pretty old for a baby: three.

"You still going on retreat?" Liz was saying.

Doris nodded. "Tomorrow. As always. You know, it's funny. I mean . . . odd. Last year Harry's mother died, and then I read in the paper two months ago that Tony Bella was dead." She looked back at Liz. "It—I don't know—it seemed as though it were some sort of symbol."

"Symbol of what?"

"I don't know . . . of the end of George and me. I mean, our props were knocked out from under us, and then—well, bad things happen in threes."

"From the ultrarational Doris Baker?"

Doris shrugged, and turned to stare at the pool. A large, mean-looking darning needle hovered over the diving board.

"How would you feel if it *were* over?" Liz was saying.

"As though part of me died. It's—listen—the first time we met I said to George, 'you're so *emotional*,' and he said, 'Why aren't you *more* emotional?' and I think our whole relationship spun around that. George . . . taught me to *be* emotional. And I suppose I taught him not to *suffer* from emotion, and the irony is that if it were over, I think I'm the one who'd be stuck with the suffering." She laughed. "He says its a habit he broke. And I think he did. Last year he was reviewing classical music for a couple of little music magazines. Struggling financially, but loving his work, and really . . . at peace."

"Hmm," Liz said, "I think I saw that movie. Bette Davis and Paul Henreid. I seem to recall it had a happy ending."

"Good," Doris said, stretching her arms. "I always adored a happy ending."

Liz was raising her Tab in a toast. "To happy endings."

Doris raised hers. "Uh-uh," she said. "To 'Be Continued.' "

FIFTEEN

"Mr. Chalmers," George said. "I thought you'd retired."

"Have," Chalmers said. "I putter, you know. Putter in the garden. Putter at the desk. Doris just got here—couple of minutes."

"Good," George said, and reached for the key.

He walked through the garden, rather nervously whistling Bach. He'd spent the morning listening to Bach. Bach and his Aristotelian logic. Every musical question answered.

"Mr. Chalmers," Doris smiled. "I thought you'd retired."

"Have," Chalmers said. "I putter, you know. Putter in the garden. Putter at the desk. George isn't here yet, if that's what you're wondering." He gave her the key.

She walked through the garden, feeling quite good, and opened the cottage; it made her smile. Nothing had changed in twenty-six years, and she remembered the year she'd begged Mr. Chalmers *not* to re-cover the fading chintz couch. He hadn't. She put her bag on the floor and considered herself in the dressing table mirror. Girdles were really remarkable things and unfairly maligned. She looked rather trim. There were roses in a vase on the coffee table; she decided to move them to the top of the piano. She'd taken piano les-

Everything tied up neatly in circles. Amazing, he thought, approaching the cottage, how music and math were so much alike. Everything ending up neat and tidy. He planned to propose such an ending to Doris: musically tidy, mathematically neat.

The trouble was, Doris couldn't carry a tune.

He opened the door.

She looked beautiful; but then she always looked beautiful. He moved across the room and kissed her, and she smelled of something delicious. He pulled back, smiling and studied her face. There were lines. He liked them. He practically knew what each of them stood for: Tony's pneumonia, Marylyn's birth, the time that Harry had almost left. . . .

sons since June and insisted on learning, to her teacher's dismay, "If I Knew You Were Coming I'd Have Baked A Cake." She played it quite terribly, but George would laugh and be terribly pleased. She rearranged the flowers and then, stepping back, stopped to admire them. Lovely. She turned.

The door opened.

He looked tired; but the sight of him gave her that old, sweet, familiar ache. She moved to his arms and they kissed, and his arms felt wonderful around her, and she still felt that wicked tingle up her spine. Dirty old lady, she thought, pleased, and looked at him. Yes, he was thinner this year. The collar of his trenchcoat was slightly frayed.

He smiled, letting go of her. "God, you feel good."

"Mmm. So do you. But you *look* tired."

He grinned. "I've been looking this way for years. You just haven't noticed."

I'd have noticed, she thought. I notice everything about you. He took off his coat; he was wearing a turtleneck sweater and slacks and he *was* thinner. . . .

"Anyway," he said, "I feel a lot better now that I'm here. This room's always had that effect on me."

"Mmm," she smiled, "I know what you mean. I guess it proves that maybe you can't *buy* happiness, but you can certainly rent it." She looked around the room. "It never changes."

"Yeah. About the only thing that doesn't."

He sat on the sofa and lit a cigarette. She was staring at him. He wasn't unaware that he looked like hell; but then he figured she'd never loved him for looks. He blew out the match. He ought to stop smoking too. But to hell with it.

She sat beside him on the couch. "In this changing world, I find that very comforting," she said.

"Yeah. Me too. He circled a finger on the worn brown chintz. "Hell, even old Chalmers is the same. Christ, he must be seventy-five by now. Remember when we first met—how even then we used to call him 'Old Chalmers'?"

She nodded.

"He must've been about the same age then as we are now."

"That," she sighed, "I do not find comforting."

He laughed. "What the hell. We were *very* young." He smiled slowly and reached for her hand. Her skin was soft.

His hand felt good. "Sometimes," she said, watching his face, "sometimes I think we've both changed a lot. And then sometimes I don't think we've changed at all."

He squinted through smoke, shaking his head. "Of course we've changed. I grew up with you." He grinned, picturing himself the way he used to be. "Remember the dumb lies I used to tell?"

She nodded, remembering the lies he used to tell. "I miss them."

"Hell," he said, "I don't. It was no fun being that insecure."

"And what about me? Have I grown up too?"

"Nope." He shook his head. "I have a feeling you were already grown-up when I met you."

"Well . . . then maybe *too* grown-up." She smiled. "You brought out the kid in me, kid."

"Tell me something?"

"Anything—shoot."

"Why is it every time I look at you, I want to put my hands all over you?"

"Oh." She kissed him, and his hands ran over her. "Yum. That's another thing that hasn't changed. You were always a sex fiend."

"Mmm." He nodded, closing his eyes, letting his fingers run up her back. "My God, you feel good. Softest thing I've touched in months is Rusty, my cocker spaniel."

"Oh?" She looked up at him frowning slightly.

Abruptly, he stood up. "How about some coffee and why don't I see if I can start this fire?" He walked to the fireplace, watching Doris from the corner of his eye. She crossed to the automatic coffee maker that had made its appearance in the cottage last year; another "free" extra provided by the management. Maybe happiness *could* be rented, he thought, but the rent was sure going up every year. He stacked some logs, and then tore up a paper saying CARTER ANNOUNCES AMNESTY PLAN, and reached for a match. "You know, I figured out with what the hell firewood costs these days, it's cheaper to buy some shoddy new furniture, break it up and then burn *it.*"

She frowned now, watching him, ignoring his tone, hearing just the words. "Honey? Are things . . . that tight?"

"No. I'm okay. I've been doing some teaching at U.C.L.A."

"Music?"

"Accounting." He poked at the fire and laughed. "It seems, with everything that's happened out there, figures are still the only things that don't lie." He moved from the fireplace, grinning wryly. "Back to a page from my youthful philosophy." He knuckled his jaw. He'd considered growing a beard again, but then he'd decided to hell with that, too.

She poured him some coffee. The line about Rusty, The Cocker Spaniel, had remained, yapping and barking, in her head. Had Helen left him? *How* could she have left him? After all this time. And when he'd never been more . . . wonderful. She set some sugar and cream on a tray.

"Why did you sell your business?" he said.

"What?" She turned. "How'd you know that?"

"I'll tell you later. What made you do it?"

"Well . . . I was bought out by a chain. It was the right offer at the right time." She put the pot and a cup on the tray and brought it to the table.

"But what do you do with yourself?" he said.

"Oh," she shrugged handing him a cup, black, with one sugar, "the usual things. Read, watch TV, play a little golf, visit my grandchildren. You know. All the jet-set stuff."

He studied her over the rim of his cup. There was something she wasn't telling him. Yet. "I thought you loved working," he said to her slowly.

She suddenly decided she wanted some coffee and made herself very busy with that. "Well, there was actually one other factor. Harry had a heart attack." She looked up quickly. "It turned out to be a mild one but he needed me to look after him, so . . ." she shrugged, and added brightly, "Anyway, it's not as if I'm in permanent retirement. There's a local election coming up in a few months and I've been approached to run."

"On what ticket?"

"Independent."

"Figures." He sat on the couch beside her, conscious again of her spicy perfume. Once, walking on a beach at Santa Barbara, he'd smelled that scent, and turned, really expecting her to be there. She hadn't been there. He sipped his coffee. "Harry okay now?"

"Oh he's just fine. Runs four miles a day and has a body like Mark Spitz." She grinned. "Unfortunately, he's still got a face like Ernest Borgnine. You want to hear a nice story about him?"

"Not . . . right now. I want to ask you something." He put down his cup. "How are you and Harry—emotionally?"

"Emotionally?" She cocked her head. "Funny, I don't

think of us as exactly . . . emotional. I'd say the answer to your question is 'comfortable.' We're comfortable."

He put down his coffee cup and knuckled his jaw, watching her. "You're willing to settle for that?"

"Oh," she shrugged. "It's not such a bad state. The word's been given a bad reputation by the young." She shrugged again, looking around the room. He'd left his raincoat on the arm of the couch; she reached for it, moving to hang it in the closet. She suddenly stopped, and realized he hadn't come in with any luggage. There were pieces in this puzzle that just didn't fit. Tony Bella was dead; maybe George couldn't stay because of Helen because George, the new George, could not tell a lie. But the softest thing that he'd touched in months was the dog?

"Where's your luggage?" she said in a casual voice. "Still in the car?"

He picked the moment to pick at a cuticle. "I—I didn't bring any luggage," he said. Now, he told himself, now or never. He took a deep breath. "I can't stay, Doris."

"Oh." She sat down. "Why?" she asked with deliberate calm.

"Look," he said, rising and starting to pace, "I've got a lot to say and a short time to say it so I'd better start now." He chewed on his lip and took another deep breath. "First of all—Helen knows about us. She's known about us for over ten years."

"Oh." Doris sighed and looked out the window. "When—uh—when did you find this out?"

"Two months ago."

"She never confronted you with it before?"

He was shaking his head.

"What made her tell you now? Was it Tony's—"

"She didn't. She didn't confront me. We have a—very close friend, Connie. Have I ever mentioned Connie before?"

Doris shook her head.

"Well, Connie told me." He paced to the piano, banged once on the keys and stared at his fist. "All these years. And she never even *hinted* she knew." Sighing, he turned again, shaking his head. He banged the piano again as he passed it, and Doris thought, this is how it ends. With a bang. "I guess that's the nicest story I've ever told about her."

Doris nodded, feeling a peculiar mix of emotions. In Helen's position would she have had the sense, and guts, to keep quiet? "Your wife's an amazing woman, George."

"She's dead."

Doris stared at him, uncomprehending.

"She died six months ago. Cancer. It was—it was all very fast."

"Oh, God." Doris felt the tears start to rise. She stood up slowly and walked to the fireplace, stared at the fire.

He watched her back, cursing himself for being so blunt; he'd handled it badly. "I'm—I'm sorry to just blurt it out like that. I just couldn't think of a—a graceful way to tell you."

She nodded, silently, facing the fire.

"You okay, honey?" he said softly.

For answer, all he got was a sigh. After a while, she said, "It's so strange. I never met Helen. But—but I feel as if I've just lost my best friend. It's—crazy." She turned. "It must have been awful for you."

He shrugged. "You cope. You don't think you can, but when you have to, you cope."

She moved to him, reaching up, stroking his face. He looked so tired. "The kids okay?"

He nodded, slowly. "Yeah. They'll survive. I don't think I could have gotten through it without them." She was watching him tenderly. George closed his eyes. Now, he told himself, now or never. "And then there was—Connie." He moved away.

"Connie?"

He fooled around with the fire. "She'd lost her husband a few years ago so there was a certain . . . empathy."

"Oh?" He was driving at something, all right. With

Number Four iron. Doris sat down, watching him move from the fire and pace.

"She's a friend, Doris. A very good friend. We've always felt very—comfortable—together. I suppose it's because she's a lot like Helen." He looked at her now. She was frowning, troubled. She was definitely troubled. "Is something the matter?"

Still frowning, she lifted her shoulders. "I—well, I just wish you'd tried to reach me."

"I did," he said quickly. "That's when I found out you'd sold the stores. I called and they gave me your home number. I dialed it. I let it ring four times and then I hung up. But it made me feel better just knowing you were there."

"I wish you'd spoken to me."

"I—well, I didn't want to intrude." He shrugged. "I didn't feel I had the right."

The words stung her. "My God, that's terrible. We should have been together."

He shrugged again, sitting beside her again; he started to pour a new round of coffee. "I've been thinking about us a lot," he said slowly. "Everything we've been through together. The things we've shared. The times we've helped each other—Did you know we've made love a hundred and thirteen times?" He smiled, self-mocking. "I figured it out on my Bomar Calculator." He poured some cream into Doris's coffee. "It's a wonderful thing to know someone that well. You know, there's *nothing* I don't know about you?—Two sugars, right?"

"No. One."

"Okay. So I don't know *everything* about you." He put the single lump of sugar in her cup and then handed it to her. "I don't know who your favorite movie stars are and I couldn't remember the name of your perfume. I spent a whole day last summer wracking my brains about that one, but I couldn't remember."

"That's funny," she smiled. "It's My Sin."

"But listen, I *do* know," he plowed right on, "that in twenty-six years, I've never been out of love with you,

Doris. I find that incredible." He took a deep breath. "So what do you say?—You want to get married?"

"Married?" she quipped. "We shouldn't even be doing *this*."

"I'm serious," he said.

She watched him. He was. She said with wonder, "You really are."

"Hell," he said, "what did you think I was—just another summer romance?"

She looked at the fire. Marrying George was the one thing she could think of that would make her happy—actually, truly, actively happy—not just 'comfortable,' not just serene. Marrying George could make her feel young, and as though a new life could begin at fifty, instead of just living out the end of the old one.

He watched her thinking; he held his breath. Finally he said, "A simple 'yes' will do."

She turned to him slowly and looked at him awhile. "There's no such thing, my love," she said gently. Shaking her head, she lowered her eyes. "How—how awfully unfair it is. If you knew how many times I've dreamed about your asking me to marry you, George. The dream has pulled me through a lot of bad times. I want—I want to thank you for that."

"And what did you say to me all those times?"

"I always said yes."

He smiled. "Then why are you hesitating now?—Hey, look," he leaned forward, "do you realize I'm giving you the opportunity to marry a man who's known you thoroughly for twenty-six years and can't walk by without grabbing your ass?"

"You always were a sweet-talker," she mused.

"Hey listen," he said, "if you don't stop me fast, I'll get serious and tell you how I feel about you, and it'll be so sweet it'll really make you sick. . . . Will you marry me?"

Doris said nothing at all.

He waited.

"I can't," she finally breathed.

"Why not?"

"I'm already married," she said.

"And you feel you have to stay with him because he needs you?"

She was shaking her head. "It's a lot of things, George. . . . Affection, respect, a sense of continuity . . . family . . . we share the same memories . . . it's—comfortable. Maybe that's what marriage is all about in the end—I don't know. . . ."

"God*damm*it!" He was up on his feet. "*I* was the one who got you back together. Good old Father O'Herlihy. Christ. Why did I *do* a stupid thing like that? I mean why was I so damned generous! Shit!"

"Because," she said softly, "you felt the same way about Helen then as the way I feel about Harry now."

"What the hell's *that* got to do with anything?"

She nodded. "If I hadn't gone back to Harry, you might have been stuck with me permanently—and you were terrified of that."

He stopped pacing, and looked at her now. He could feel a sheepish grin on his face, starting to spread. He nodded slowly. "You could always see through me, couldn't you?"

"Well . . . that's okay. I always liked what I saw."

"Well, I want you now."

"You can still have me. Once a year. Same time, same place." She looked at him, standing there, shaking his head. "What is it?" she said.

He was pacing again, chewing his lip. "Doris," he said, and then stopped; he paced; he was rubbing his jaw; he pulled at his ear. "Doris—I—I need a wife. I'm just not the kind of man who can live alone. I want you to marry me but when I came here I knew there was a chance you'd say no. What I'm trying to say is—without you, I'll—I'll probably end up marrying Connie. No, that's a lie. I will marry Connie. She knows all about you. And the point is, she's just not the kind of a woman who would—go along with the situation. I suppose what I'm saying is, that if you don't marry me—we won't ever see each other again." He turned and looked at her.

Doris was very quietly crying.

He reached for her hand. "Honey, what's the matter?"

"The—the thought of never seeing you again—it *terrifies* me."

"*Doris, for God's sake—marry me!*"

"I—" she sat there crying," I—I *can't*."

He looked away. In one more second, he was going to start crying himself.

"Don't . . . hate me," she said.

"Oh God. I couldn't hate you. I was just trying to think of something that would break your heart, make you really bawl, and make you decide to come away with me."

"Well," she sniffed, "you know us Italians. We never cry."

"Yeah." He stood. She was already back in control of herself. "Well," he said quickly, "I have to catch a plane. What time is it?"

She tried to look at her watch, but her eyes were still too misty with tears. She held out her wrist to him.

"Six-o-five?"

"No." She sniffed again. "Two thirty. I always keep my watch three hours and thirty-five minutes fast."

He was definitely going to cry. "How long have you been doing that?"

"Twenty-six years."

"Why would anyone do that?" he asked, in wonder

"Personal idiosyncrasy," she said.

"Yeah . . . well . . ." He gave her a long, Fina Look; then he kissed her a Final Kiss. He pulled awa and looked at her again. He started for the door, an stopped in the doorway. "Who *were* your favorit movie stars?"

"Lon McAllister," she said slowly, "and Howar Keel, Cary Grant, Marlon Brando, and Laurence Oliv ier."

He grinned at the list. "You've come a long way."

"We both have."

"Yeah." He remembered his raincoat. She'd droppe

it on the chair. He reached for it, moving again to the door. "Always keep your watch three hours and twenty-five minutes fast, huh?"

She nodded, gulping.

"I—I can't believe this is happening to us. . . ." He could feel tears coming; he let one fall before he turned, very quickly, and walked through the door.

He walked through the garden, expecting—no, hoping—he'd turn around and see her, find her running after him.

He turned.

She wasn't there.

All that was there was an empty garden.

Only the garden wasn't empty at all.

It was filled with her—years of her—everywhere he looked.

He could see her, standing, pregnant, by the pond; she stretched up to kiss him.

"*What's that for?*"

"*Being nice. Asking Chalmers to go to the movies.*"

"*Hell, I just figured it might take two of us to navigate you into the seat of a car.*"

She sighed, and leaned her back against a tree. "*Some day, before you're old and gray, you will learn to take a compliment by just saying thank you.*"

"*Don't look now, but I'm old and gray. . . .*"

He stopped, lit a cigarette, and blew out the match. Through the smoke he watched her stalk through the garden, wearing that beaded Indian headband, long dark hair swinging to her waist. She was scowling at him, but she suddenly smiled and ran to him, running a hand down his face.

"*When did I suddenly become so appealing?*"

"*Mmm. When you went from pompous to confused.*" *She grinned at him.* "*Okay. So what's your pleasure? A good book, a walk by the ocean, or me?*"

"You," he chose again, and passed by the porch, glancing through the open doors of the restaurant and off to the table in the corner where she sat in a bright blue suit and a silly straw hat studying a menu.

"You," he chose again, kicking a stone, and watching it jump ahead of him, straight down the path that led to the parking lot and Doris—in satin lounging pajamas, pulling a picnic basket out of the trunk of a shiny '72 MG.

He turned, and she was drumming her nails on the wheel of a dark blue '56 Nash coupé.

"I just don't see any point in going on." She ran a hand quickly through short blond hair. "That's why I think we should just break it off."

"My God, you're really serious."

"I've always been serious. . . ."

He walked to his car.

"Well . . . good night, George. I have to go."

"Do you really have to go?"

"I really have to go—you better get off the running board, George. . . ."

He winced, tossed his cigarette down to the ground, and crushed it into the gravel with his heel. He looked back quickly, across the garden to Cottage Seven. He could see her now, standing by the window, watching him: That was all she could do. That was all it was fair to *ask* her to do. He shouldn't have asked her for anything more. She couldn't do it. He knew she couldn't. He'd gambled and lost.

Sighing, he opened the door of the car.

She stopped watching when he opened the car. She didn't want to see him driving away; didn't want to know he was driving away for the last time. The Last Time. It wasn't possible. Yes, it was. In another minute, George would be gone. Forever. Impossible.

She turned from the window.

And George wasn't gone. He was in the room, with her, pacing it, wearing a jacket and a shoe.

"Dorothy—first of all I want you to know that last night was the most beautiful, fantastic. . . ."

He would always be there inside this room that was inside her head; impossible to lose him. She walked to the bed where she'd left her handbag and lit a cigarette. She was still crying. Seven balloons were tied to the bed.

Orange crepe paper streamed from the mantel; a sign said, HAPPY ANNIVERSARY, DARLING, and George said, pointing down at the cake: *"Make a wish."*

She nodded, and blew out the match.

"What did you wish?"

"I have only one wish."

"What?"

"That you keep showing up every year. . . ."

She shook her head slowly. There were no more years. They'd run out of years. How could that have happened?

Connie?

If she started to think about Connie, she would get irational, and that wasn't fair.

It wasn't fair to expect George to give up the rest f his life for the sake of a single weekend a year.

It wasn't fair to ask Connie to understand.

It wasn't fair to leave Harry with a bitter ending.

And it wasn't fair to have to be fair.

"Was that a proposal?" he asked softly.

"You interested?"

"Are you?"

"I always thought we'd make a nice couple. . . ."

She walked to the piano and vaguely one-fingered eir stupid song.

"Other people would get 'Be My Love.' "

My love, she thought, my love, my love . . . and ran, suddenly weeping, to the bed.

"Okay, goddammit!" He burst through the door, carying a suitcase. "Okay, I'm back." Scowling, he dropped is bag and glared at her.

"B-but wh-what," she stammered, starting to rise, w-what about Connie?"

"Connie?" he glowered. "There *is* no Connie. I made er up. No, goddammit. That's a lie, too. There *is* a onnie, but she's eighty years old!"

"Darling . . . ?"

He was throwing his raincoat on the bed. "Oh Christ," e grumbled, "I wanted you to *marry* me, and I figured f you thought there was somebody else, you'd—look, okay, I didn't think it through, but I was *desperate,* really *desperate,* see?"

She started to giggle through leftover tears.

He glared at her. "Dammit, it isn't funny. For once in my life, I just wanted a happy ending, okay? Okay, so forget about happy endings. I'm here and all I know is I'll keep coming back till our bones are too brittle to risk contact!"

"Oh, honey." Her laughter had turned back to tears as she moved to his arms and held him very tight.

Gently, he cupped her chin in his hands and lifted it. "Why are you crying now?"

"Because," she said, crying, "I just . . . love . . . happy endings."

Beryl Bainbridge

'A brilliantly talented writer.' *Times*. 'It is a joy to find writers with the skill and observation of Miss Bainbridge.' *Daily Mirror*. 'Alarming humour . . . a powerful talent.' *Sunday Telegraph*

A Quiet Life

Sweet William

The Dressmaker

The Bottle Factory Outing

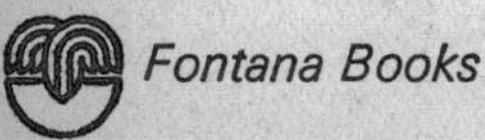

Fontana Paperbacks

Fontana is a leading paperback publisher of fiction and non-fiction, with authors ranging from Alistair MacLean, Agatha Christie and Desmond Bagley to Solzhenitsyn and Pasternak, from Gerald Durrell and Joy Adamson to the famous Modern Masters series.

In addition to a wide-ranging collection of internationally popular writers of fiction, Fontana also has an outstanding reputation for history, natural history, military history, psychology, psychiatry, politics, economics, religion and the social sciences.

All Fontana books are available at your bookshop or newsagent; or can be ordered direct. Just fill in the form and list the titles you want.

FONTANA BOOKS, Cash Sales Department, G.P.O. Box 29, Douglas, Isle of Man, British Isles. Please send purchase price, plus 8p per book. Customers outside the U.K. send purchase price, plus 10p per book. Cheque, postal or money order. No currency.

NAME (Block letters)

ADDRESS

While every effort is made to keep prices low, it is sometimes necessary to increase prices on short notice. Fontana Books reserve the right to show new retail prices on covers which may differ from those previously advertised in the text or elsewhere.